To Cheryl
I pray yo
Blessings!
Misty M Beller

ry!

SAVING THE MOUNTAIN MAN'S LEGACY

BROTHERS OF SAPPHIRE RANCH
BOOK EIGHT

MISTY M. BELLER

Misty M. Beller
BOOKS

"For My thoughts are not your thoughts,
Nor are your ways My ways," says the Lord.

"For as the heavens are higher than the earth,
So are My ways higher than your ways,
And My thoughts than your thoughts.

Isaiah 55:8-9 (NKJV)

CHAPTER 1

*A*lmost to the mine.

As Sampson Coulter's horse neared the last curve in the trail, he straightened in his saddle, stretching out his back. After working so many months in McPharland's cave mines, his body had forgotten how it felt to spend hours in the saddle. He should have left Missoula Mills earlier yesterday. Then he wouldn't have had to stop for the night in that old trapper's cabin. At least he'd had shelter before the rest of today's long ride.

Now he barely had time to check in with Mick, hitch the horses quickly, and get back to Jedidiah with the wagon load he'd been sent to retrieve. He didn't relish sleeping in the cold again, especially with the blasting powder packed in the wagon bed, but he'd have to if he didn't want to drive through the night. That stuff became unreliable in icy temperatures.

As the trees opened up around him, he raised a hand to shield his eyes from the bright light reflecting off the snow around the mountain that hid McPharland's mine. Even though the sun shone high overhead, the cold wind bit through his coat and sent chills up his spine. It wouldn't be long now until the snow started falling.

And Christmas. A pang gripped his chest, one he usually didn't allow in. He'd lost track of the exact day, but someone in Missoula Mills had said Christmas was later this week.

This was the first yuletide he'd be away from his family. They'd have a festive time, with the place all decorated with holly and ribbons and a tree. The women would make a big meal, and there'd be presents. Singing.

He pushed hard against the memories, forcing his mind onto the terrain around him.

A strange noise sounded, and for a second, it felt like part of his imaginings. His family singing carols.

But this wasn't singing. A cry, maybe. Not a fox or any kind of wildcat.

Was that...a baby?

Another cry confirmed the sound. What on earth? It didn't come from the direction of the mountain. To the right of it maybe.

His mind whirled with possibilities, and he turned his horse that direction. Approaching the source of the noise, he slowed his mount.

A small wagon came into view, partially hidden by a cluster of pine trees. A young woman stood beside it, her back turned to him as she bent over something in the wagon bed.

The baby's cries grew louder, and the woman's voice rose in frustration. "Shh, shh, little one. I know, I know. Just give me a moment."

Sampson pulled his horse to a halt a few steps away and dismounted. "Ma'am? Is everything all right?"

The woman spun, her eyes wide.

He took her in, the force of her appearance—such a small,

dainty thing out here in this wilderness tainted so fully by McPharland's presence—caught him off guard. He braced his feet to keep from backing up a step.

She stared back, mirroring his shock. Then the babe wailed, and her attention snapped to the child on the wagon. The lower half of the child had been stripped bare. That explained the crying and kicking its little legs. The infant must be half frozen in this wind.

The woman wrestled to cover the babe with a strip of unwieldy cloth. "I just...it won't... Be still, Ruby. We have to get you..."

She seemed to be having a rough time of it, with one hand firm on a little leg and the other trying to wrap the fabric around the child.

He moved to her side, keeping enough space between them that she hopefully wouldn't think him a threat. "How can I help?" He'd never put on a diaper before, but he could offer an extra set of hands.

She spared the quickest of glances his way, but a fresh wail from the child made her cringe. She spoke loudly to be heard over the cries. "Can you hold her feet? Gently. She keeps squirming, and I don't want to get the clean diaper soiled."

He reached in to grip the tiny ankles in one fist. How had he never realized how massive his hands were? But the moment his calloused fingers closed around those toothpick ankles, he added his other hand. He couldn't grip them tight. This babe was barely bigger than his palms, and her ankles weren't much larger around than his thumb. Any little squeeze might snap the bones in two.

The woman worked around his gangly arms, wrapping the cloth in a neat hold that hadn't seemed possible when she was fighting with the material seconds ago. As she pulled the knot tight, she murmured, "Keep hold of her another minute while I get the rest of it off."

He checked the pressure of his grip as the woman worked the babe's tiny hands out of her sleeves. Did she intend to strip the child fully? It was too cold out here for all that. This infant couldn't be more than a few days old. How could she even survive being so tiny?

But when the woman turned the babe's shoulders to release the back of the gown underneath her, a wave of stench wafted up. Ugh.

Turning away, he pressed his mouth closed and tried not to breathe through his nose. That diaper must not have done its job well at all.

"You can let go now," the woman said. "Thank you."

Whew. Thank goodness. He released the babe's ankles and stepped back. Once more, he turned his head for a clean breath, but that gust of smell must have singed his nose hairs. He couldn't get shed of the odor.

"That's my girl. All better." The woman murmured quiet words as she lifted the babe up to her shoulder, tucking the blanket around her.

He could no longer see the infant, but her cries turned to shuddering whimpers. The sound twisted something inside him. Such a fragile, helpless little thing.

The woman swayed and bounced, whispering something he couldn't hear. Then she lifted her eyes to him, a hint of embarrassment tinging them. "Thank you for your help."

He nodded, then shuffled back a step and glanced around. "Your man gone somewhere?" He'd not thought of that before. Why were these two here alone? And so close to Mick's mine? Surely her husband didn't work for Sampson's employer.

Mick didn't take on families. Only single men who could live in the bunk room and work in the caves.

She lifted her chin, but it did little to raise her stature. She must be a head and a half shorter than he was. Not even five foot if he had to guess. "I'm looking for my father. He works near here."

His body tensed, but he kept his face casual. "What's his name?" She had to be talking about Mick's operation. Was her father Cornwall, the new fellow who came a fortnight ago? He didn't seem old enough to have a grown daughter, though this woman didn't look much older than a girl herself.

She was scrutinizing him. Wondering what kind of men her father worked with? "Jedidiah Hampton."

He blinked, the reaction slipping out before he could stop it. Jedidiah...Hampton?

Surely, she didn't mean the tyrant whom McPharland depended on to do his dirty work. Had he ever heard Jedidiah's surname? Apparently not, as Hampton wasn't familiar at all.

Just *Jedidiah*, like the first man had only been named Adam. Except Adam had been breathed to life by the Almighty, and Jedidiah had probably been created directly by Satan himself. He delighted in evil more than any person Sampson had ever met.

The woman studied him, so he tried to clear any remnants of shock from his expression and raised his brows. "What does he look like exactly?"

She frowned and gave a half-shrug. "I don't know. Taller than me but..." She glanced above Sampson's eyes. "Not near as tall as you. Hair darker than mine but with gray mixed in."

That wasn't a very detailed description. It described Jedidiah though. How many men by that name could there be in this area? But... "You say you're his daughter?"

Jedidiah always seemed more demon than human. How could he possibly have a child? Or rather...how could he have sired a young woman as pretty as this one?

But if she truly was her father's daughter, she must be wily. Devious. Innocent in appearance but capable of great evil. He'd best be on guard.

And he should also make certain they were speaking of the same man.

Once more, he worked for a casual tone. "I know a man named Jedidiah, but I don't know his surname. Do you know whose mine your father works in?"

McPharland possessed the only mine in this area, as far as he knew, but this woman might have gotten off track in her search.

She squinted. "A man named Mick?" It came out as a question, as though she needed him to say for sure.

His middle churned. Her words confirmed all he needed.

He let his gaze roam her face. She did have the same small, condensed features as Jedidiah. On her, they looked delicate and lovely, though on her father, they only made him blend in with a crowd. Like an old miner who's outlived his prime.

Her eyes were different than her father's though, wide and clear blue. Jedidiah's were dark and narrowed. Or maybe that was simply from the constant glare he gave everyone he deigned to speak to.

The babe on her shoulder fussed again, and the woman resumed swaying. "Can you tell me where I can find my father?"

Sampson sent a glance toward the mountain. No one had come out, and they were mostly hidden from view, but that didn't mean a guard wasn't watching. If this truly was Jedidiah's daughter, he might be using her to prove Sampson's loyalty. He'd need to do as she asked, as much as he thought Jedidiah would want anyway. Certainly, he couldn't allow her to interfere with his orders, but letting her ride along behind him wouldn't slow him down.

"I just left your father in Missoula Mills. He sent me back for supplies. It will take me about a half hour to hitch the team and load up, then you can follow me back to him if you'd like. It's a full day's ride, and since we're starting at midday, we'll need to stay the night on the road. There's a little trapper's cabin I usually bed down in. It's a bit drafty, but we can start a fire and keep warm."

As he spoke, the reality of what he was suggesting settled in. She had a newborn baby. It couldn't be healthy for the child to spend so many hours in the cold, then sleep in a shack that barely kept out the wind. And the woman... How long since she'd given birth? Could she even drive a team?

And the biggest question of all...where was her husband?

He looked around, thinking he'd see a man in the scrubby trees, but nobody emerged. "Is your husband close by? I can wait a little while, or else give you directions to the main road."

Her pert chin tipped up. "I'm not married. But if you'll give me those directions, I won't hold you up any longer."

Not married.

The words sunk like a weight around his shoulders. He couldn't let her go alone. Especially not with that tiny bundle in her arms.

He needed to get her to Jedidiah. And he had to get the powder there quickly.

He glanced at her wagon. She didn't have much loaded in it —just a few crates and a rocking chair. He could probably fit them in the wagon with the blasting powder. Except the rocking chair. He couldn't lay anything heavy on the powder, so that would have to stay.

"I'll tell you what. Let me get my team and wagon ready, then we'll move your things into mine, and I can drive both of you. That way you can have your hands free to take care of Little Bit there." He nodded to the babe, who'd begun to make little mewling noises.

The woman frowned. "I'd rather take my wagon. If you'll just tell me how to get there, I'll be on my way."

He fought to hold in his sigh. "I can tell you, ma'am, but Jedidiah would not look on me kindly for sending his daughter and grandbaby off into the wilderness on their own. 'Specially when I'm headed the same way with a wagon that has plenty of room for you both."

She added a pinched mouth to her frown. "I don't want to be a bother."

Was there a polite way to say how much more frustrating she was being keeping him standing here when he had a schedule to keep? His brother Gil could have managed it, but Sampson would do best not to try. He did offer a smile. "I'd appreciate you letting me help, ma'am, your father being Jedidiah and all."

That last bit seemed to bring her around, for she finally sighed. "All right then. Should I follow you with my team?"

He shook his head. "Stay here and get your things packed up. I'll be back soon."

He'd better make up all the time he could, for surely traveling with a woman and babe would slow him down. And he didn't relish Jedidiah's reaction if he kept the man waiting.

CHAPTER 2

$\mathcal{G}$race Hampton's heart pounded against her ribs. Was it really a good idea to travel with a man she'd just met? Leave her own wagon and team behind, putting her and Ruby at his mercy?

If he was as trustworthy as he seemed, she would be much better off not having to worry about handling the team. And he was Father's employee.

But she would need the wagon and horses to start her new life once she spoke with her father. Maybe what the man needed to carry could be packed in her rig.

He didn't return right away, so she used the time to dress Ruby. "I'm sorry I kept you in the blanket so long, sweet one." She pulled on the babe's long-sleeved undergarment and her flannel gown before swaddling her again in the blanket—this time far more securely than before.

All their belongings were still packed, so she should be ready for whatever they decided to do when he brought his wagon.

Her only other choice would be to follow his wagon with her own rig, driving and caring for Ruby as best she could. That meant Ruby would have to lie in her basket most of the time.

Then she'd have to stop the wagon to feed her. The trip would take longer than the day he'd said.

And now that the weather had turned cold, she needed to find her father as quickly as possible, get enough money to live on for a little while, and find a safe place for them to settle.

She worked to still her whirling thoughts. Whatever it took to reach her father, she had to do it quickly. Even if that included riding with this stranger for a day.

Besides, she wasn't completely defenseless. In addition to the revolver she had tucked in the hidden pocket of her skirt, she also had the rifle. She wouldn't hesitate to pull either weapon if she needed to protect herself and Ruby.

The crunching of wagon wheels across the ground sounded behind her, and she turned to see two horses pulling a wagon into view. One of the animals had the same coloring as one of the horses that pulled Oren's wagon—brown with black mane and tail.

This wasn't her old delivery driver, though, but the man she'd met earlier driving the team. He halted them when his wagon was alongside hers. A number of crates filled part of his wagon bed, but there looked to be enough room in her rig to hold them.

She forced confidence into her tone. "I won't be coming back this direction, so I need to take my wagon and team. Will your supplies fit in my wagon?"

He set his brake and eyed her load, then his. "Looks like it might." He jumped to the ground, then started hauling the boxes from his bed and positioned them in her wagon. Thankfully, she'd kept her load to a minimum.

She'd debated over what to bring, ending up packing most of their clothes and blankets and food, as well as a few books. She'd not known whether she should bring furniture or not. It seemed like each house would have its own, so carrying hers would be a waste. But then, she'd never purchased a new house, nor rented a room, so she hadn't been sure. Mama's rocker was the one piece that felt like it belonged more to Grace than to their house.

She settled Ruby in her basket and untied the goat from behind her wagon. "Come on, Camelot. The grass is just as good over here." The nanny had begun eating the moment they stopped and complained with a *maa* as Grace tugged her away from the underbrush so she could tie the rope to the man's wagon.

All the while, she kept an eye on the man.

He moved efficiently, no sign of strain as he hefted his crates into her wagon and moved her belongings around. Belongings that had taken every bit of her strength to push up into the bed. It was hard to gauge his character from his actions, but he seemed focused and purposeful. Efficient, not sparing a glance her way as he arranged the items to fit.

Everything fit neatly, just as he'd said, with his cargo taking up only a portion of the wagon bed. He'd tucked her belongings around the outer edges. He held her mother's rocking chair in his arms as he studied the load.

Then he leaned over the side and placed it on the ground. "We'll need to leave the chair here. I can put it in your father's room, so you can come back for it or work out a way with him to get it." He spoke casually, already jumping down to carry the chair to his wagon.

"No." The word flew out before she could temper it. She inhaled a breath to steady herself. "I can't leave the chair behind. Just put it on top of the boxes."

He shook his head. "Nothing can go on top of these crates. They're too fragile."

Frustration welled in her chest. Why was he being so difficult? "You need to figure something else out then, because I'm not leaving my mother's rocking chair. I need it for the baby."

The man frowned. "You can get it when you come back this way."

"I'm not planning to come back." Grace fought to keep her voice steady, though it trembled with emotion. "That rocking chair is one of the few things of my mother's I have left. I'd sooner drive my own wagon than leave it behind."

For a long moment, he simply stared at her, his expression unreadable. Then, with a sigh, he carried the chair back to her wagon. After studying a few seconds, he tied it to the back of the bench, positioned above the bed so it rested on none of the crates.

Relief flooded through Grace. Perhaps he wasn't as heartless as he seemed. When he finished, he drove his team away to park the wagon and pasture the horses.

Ruby had started her hungry cry, the sign she wouldn't be held off from food much longer.

"All right then." Grace picked up the wicker basket by its two woven handles, making faces at the babe as she carried her to the front of their wagon. "I have a feeding bottle ready for you. I know you're hungry."

Ruby's cries eased into a shuddering sob as she studied Grace's face, those wide blue eyes so desperate. "You're so pitiful when you're hungry."

She placed the basket on the bench and hauled herself up, positioning it between her and where the man would sit. The babe would be a nice buffer.

By the time he returned, she had the babe cradled in her arms, the feeding bottle's rubber nipple between her rosebud lips. Ruby drank hungrily, her eyes closed and jaw working as she suckled.

The man didn't speak, just strode around to his side of the wagon and stepped up to the seat. He gave Ruby a sideways look as he settled, taking up the reins. Then he focused ahead, released the brake, and shook the reins. "Walk on."

The wagon lurched into motion, and she braced her feet against the buckboard, gripping Ruby tightly as they started off.

As the wagon rolled along the rutted ground, she sneaked glances at the man beside her. He kept his gaze fixed forward, his hands steady. The silence stretched between them, broken only by the creaking of the wagon, the click of the horses' hooves on rocks, and the occasional snuffle from Ruby as she drank.

Finally, Grace cleared her throat. "I don't believe I caught your name."

"Sampson. Sampson Coulter, ma'am." He looked at her briefly before returning his attention to the road.

"Well, Mr. Coulter, I appreciate you giving us a ride." She shifted Ruby in her arms to reposition the bottle.

"No trouble." His tone was polite but distant. "And you are…?"

"Grace Hampton."

He shot her a look, brows lowered. "Hampton is your… married name?"

A question she should have expected, and he must have realized exactly what he was asking, for he jerked his focus back to the horses. "Never mind. It's nice to meet you, Mrs. Hampton."

With Hampton being her father's name, he was no doubt thinking she must have lied about something.

Best she set him straight. And consider changing her name if she planned to raise Ruby as her own. Or…maybe that wouldn't be necessary, for soon she wouldn't be around people who knew her father.

She sat a little straighter. "*Miss* Hampton. I'm not married. Ruby isn't my daughter by birth, but she was given to me to raise." She motioned to the feeding bottle. "Thus the reason we travel with a goat and this feeder."

Mr. Coulter eyed her once more, then his gaze dipped down to Ruby. "Someone gave you their child? Forever?"

His tone made a smile tug at her cheeks, though the situation held no humor. "I…well, yes. I think so."

His focus returned to her face, his brows lifting. "You *think* so?"

Heat flared through her, and she fought to keep from stammering. "Yes. I mean…*yes*." Now she couldn't keep her flush down. She huffed out a breath. "She was left on my doorstep. I came outside one afternoon and there lay this basket, with Ruby inside, and a box of blankets and diapers. Even this bottle and the goat."

She sent Mr. Coulter a glare. "So yes, I'm assuming they meant for me to raise her as my own. No one's been back for her, so she and I are carrying on like this will be forever."

She glanced down at the cherubic face that had immediately latched hold of her heart. After two weeks and everything they'd been through together, she couldn't imagine having to turn the babe back over to someone else. And if the *someone* was who she thought it was, she didn't anticipate being asked to give Ruby back.

Mr. Coulter still stared at her, and now his jaw had dropped open a little, just enough to reveal the shadows of his lower teeth.

She fought a giggle. This big strapping man had been thoroughly stunned speechless. Well, that made two of them.

At last, he found his voice. "Some stranger just abandoned their child with you? And you never found out who?"

She shrugged, looking down at Ruby's peaceful face. "I have my suspicions. But I never saw him again."

"Did you not try to find them? Make them take responsibility?" His voice rose with indignation.

"I understood why they did it." Grace kept her tone soft, though her heart clenched. "They needed help. And I'm glad to give it. Ruby will have the best care I can provide." And all the love she could ever want.

He shook his head, turning back to the road. "Ain't right, leaving a babe like that. Anything could've happened to her."

Grace lifted her chin. "But it didn't. And she has me now."

Mr. Coulter turned quiet again, but not very long this time. "So that's why you're looking for your father."

Something in his tone made her bristle. "I need to move closer to town where I can have...access to things. I only wanted to let him know I'd be leaving." That wasn't quite true. She needed money, something she and Mama had never had to worry over. But they'd also never needed to leave the little house in the valley.

He snorted, a sound that unsettled something in her middle.

She waited for him to explain, but he remained silent. Should she ask what that meant? Maybe she didn't want to know.

And really, did she need his opinion? He knew nothing of her and her life, nor did he need to.

She settled back on the bench and tipped the bottle higher so Ruby could get the last of the milk. All she had to do now was care for her sweet daughter and count the hours until she reached the next step in their new life.

CHAPTER 3

*S*ampson guided the wagon off the main road as dusk fell around them. Finally. His weary bones craved a stop for the night. The path through the trees was short, and he reined the team to a stop beside the old trapper's shack.

Once he'd set the brake and climbed down, he moved around to assist Miss Hampton. She gathered the baby close before placing her hand in his, allowing him to help her navigate the steep step. Once she stood steady on the ground, he reached for the woven basket that served as the babe's bed. "I'll bring this in, then fetch the rest of what we need for the night."

Miss Hampton's eyes darted over the dilapidated cabin. She looked uncertain, but they had little choice. They needed shelter for the night.

He pushed open the door and glanced in to make sure the place was vacant. The interior was dim, but enough light came in through the doorway and the cracks in the walls he could see the space. A stone fireplace stood on the far wall with a stack of wood beside it. Otherwise, the single room stood empty.

He stepped aside for Miss Hampton to enter, then followed her in and placed the basket on the floor where they'd lay out the bedrolls. "I'll be back to start the fire soon." That would give them light. The woman didn't seem bothered by the dim interior, just crouched in front of the babe as he left.

It didn't take long to gather blankets, his food bag, and the satchel she'd asked him to bring inside. When he stepped back into the cabin, Miss Hampton had laid the babe on a blanket spread on the floor. She was doing something with the child's clothes, cooing and murmuring as she worked.

He set about starting a fire in the hearth to chase away the bitter chill seeping through the log walls. He had half a ham and a few biscuits from the cafe in Missoula Mills, which they could eat cold. It'd be nice to have a warm meal though, something to heat their insides. Good thing he'd brought along a frying pan.

Within a few minutes, the flames crackled nicely. He sat back on his heels to watch the blaze. Something about a fire in the hearth always made a room cozier, even a shack like this one.

"I can cook a meal for us." Miss Hampton's voice sounded behind him.

He turned to see that she'd stood, leaving the babe on the blanket but wrapped up tight again.

She waited for his answer, hesitation raising her brows. With the fire's glow like that, he couldn't miss how pretty her features were. Almost like an angel.

He motioned toward his food bag. "I was just going to fry up some ham to eat with biscuits. If you can stand that fare, I've got it covered."

She gave a single nod. "That sounds nice. Could you keep an eye on Ruby while I go to the wagon? She should lie there and play."

Now it was his turn to widen his eyes. He had no idea what to do if she started crying. But the babe held a piece of braided leather and seemed calm enough. He nodded, despite the nerves tightening inside him. "Sure."

Miss Hampton strode out the door. *Lord, help me.* But surely Miss Hampton wouldn't have left if there would be trouble.

He pulled the skillet from his bag and set it on the hearth to heat. Then he opened the cloth that held the food. The ham would taste mighty fine fried up crisp.

As he laid the pieces in the pan, a strange squawk came from the floor behind him. He glanced over his shoulder to see the babe staring at him, eyes wide and curious.

"You doing all right there, little bit?" Speaking to a newborn felt like talking to himself, especially when she made no sound in return.

"All right then. I'll just finish getting this food ready to cook." He turned back to his work but shifted so he could still see her at the corner of his gaze.

Funny how the little thing seemed to be studying him, watching his every move. Didn't seem natural for a babe so tiny to be that alert. He moved the pan into the fire, positioning it where the ham should fry without burning.

A wail split the quiet. He jumped, nearly dropping the knife in his other hand. He spun to see the child crying, her little face scrunched up in a howl.

He placed his knife on the hearth and watched the door, wiping his hands on the edge of the cloth that had held the food. Miss Hampton must have heard the cry. She'd come back to help the babe.

Wouldn't she?

Another howl echoed through the room, making his heart pound. Surely, the woman would run back inside any moment now.

But she didn't. The door stayed closed. And the babe loosed another squall, this time longer than the others.

Tension thrummed through his veins. He had to do something. He couldn't leave her crying there without help.

Setting the pan aside, he grabbed the cloth that had held the biscuits and wiped his hands again. Then he pushed up from his crouch and moved the few steps to kneel beside the newborn's blanket. Was she in pain? Sick? Had an insect crept in and bit her? His imagination took off on a dark path, thinking of of all the perils that could befall a person in an abandoned cabin like this one.

He bent low, trying to keep his voice soft. "What is it, little bit?" As soon as the words left his lips, the ruckus ceased. Her mouth still hung open in the shape of a wail, but her wide, teary eyes stared up at him.

For a long moment, they simply looked at each other. Was there pain in her expression? Not that he could tell.

Then she squeezed her eyes shut and loosed another howl.

"Hey now, no need for all that." He reached out a tentative hand to pat her belly. "Your mama will be back soon."

The babe quieted again and blinked up at him, tears clinging to her lashes. Her chin still trembled, but she seemed to be listening to him.

He'd best keep talking. But what should he say to a baby?

She whimpered, and he started blathering about dinner. "Are you hungry? I've got some good ham frying up. In fact, it might just burn if I don't turn the slices."

Her mouth settled into a normal line, and her curious gaze stayed on him.

He didn't dare move away yet. Not even to take his hand from her middle. "I'll put biscuits in the pan to warm with the grease from the ham. They'll be as dandy as if we had fresh butter. Don't wanna cook 'em too long though or they'll be dry."

The babe reached for his hand with one tiny fist. She gripped his pinky and tugged, so he let her pull him. The contact warmed something inside him. How peculiar. She was so small, so easy to break. Yet she held him in a grip he would have to pry himself away from. If he had any desire to do so.

"I see you two are getting acquainted."

He jerked up at Miss Hampton's voice. He'd not even heard the door open.

She stood just inside, a soft smile on her face in the dim light from the fire.

He gave a sheepish look and tried to pull his finger away, but the babe still held on fiercely. "She's, um, got my finger. She was crying, and talking seemed to help. Then she grabbed hold and…"

Miss Hampton stepped closer and crouched by the baby's head. "I think she likes you."

He snorted, even as the idea spread heat through his entire body.

Miss Hampton spoke again, this time to the babe. "I know, sweet pea. But Mr. Coulter needs to do his own work." She reached out to slide the babe's hand from his finger, her skin brushing against his. The contact sent a tingle up his arm. He'd touched her before without event—when he'd helped her down from wagon.

Maybe taking care of the babe had addled his mind. Time to get back to the fire, where he belonged.

He moved to the hearth, pushing away all those strange feelings. The ham sizzled in the pan, and he turned the pieces to brown the other side. Thankfully, they hadn't burned. He placed the biscuits in the rendered fat to warm, just as he'd told the babe he would. The simple domestic task settled his nerves. This was familiar territory.

Behind him, Miss Hampton hummed a soft tune. The gentle melody mixed with the crackle of the fire and filled the small space. He glanced over his shoulder to see her lift the child— Wasn't her name Ruby?—into her arms and sway in a soothing motion.

Ruby nestled against Miss Hampton's shoulder, her tiny hand clutching the fabric of the woman's shirt. The scene looked so natural, so right. A protectiveness surged through him, something he'd never felt so strongly. He wanted to keep them safe, to shelter them from the cruel world outside these walls.

But it wasn't his place. He turned back to the fire and drew a steadying breath. Miss Hampton wasn't his responsibility. He'd offered to help her get to Missoula. Once they arrived, she'd be back under her father's protection.

The thought almost made him spit. Jedidiah was no protector. He was a bully. A lunatic. A man without a soul.

How could he turn this woman and innocent child over to him? Surely, she knew what kind of a man her father was. Did that mean Miss Hampton approved of his actions? Or maybe she didn't know the extent of his evil. Probably she *didn't*.

It didn't seem possible she could have been raised by a man and not influenced by his lousy moral code—or lack of one. She seemed gentle and kind, though they'd only met. Could she be hiding a rougher side?

Sampson searched through his memories. He'd never heard Jedidiah mention a family. Jedidiah lived at the mine, so Sampson knew Miss Hampton hadn't shared a home with her father recently. He would have seen her. And he'd never pictured Jedidiah as a family man. Nothing domestic about that slimy weasel.

Once the food was ready, he pulled the frying pan from the heat and set it on a cool part of the hearth. "Help yourself. I'll go milk the goat."

"I've already done it." Miss Hampton crouched to place Ruby on the blanket.

He straightened. "You did?" How had she managed that in the few minutes she was outside? It must have been longer than he realized.

"She milks quickly. I needed to start her grazing too." Miss Hampton stood and eyed the food with a look that said she'd probably been hungry a while.

He stepped away from the fireplace. "Help yourself. I didn't think to pack plates." When he'd stopped by the bunk room in the cave, he'd thrown the pan and some cornmeal into his bag to make johnny cakes in the morning, but he'd forgotten to add something to flip the cakes with. Hopefully, a knife could do for that. Meeting this woman and baby so far from civilization and so close to the mine...it had thrown him off course in a way he still hadn't quite recovered from.

She motioned from him to the food. "You eat first. I can wait."

He shook his head and started for the door. "I need to unhitch the team and feed them. I'll be a few minutes, so eat without me and get settled in for the night."

He should also bring in more firewood. Maybe by the time he returned, they'd be asleep and he could bed down himself. But first, he needed some fresh air to clear his head.

This trip was not turning out at all the way he'd expected.

CHAPTER 4

*G*race's foot tapped out a rhythm on the floor of the wagon as she watched the snow-patched landscape pass by.

She'd never been to this part of the country, but it looked like every other stretch of land they'd passed through that morning. Trees lining both sides of the road, and snowcapped mountains rising in all directions.

The only difference was that her father was nearby.

Her chest tightened at the thought of seeing him. He wouldn't be happy about her leaving the house. Nor surprising him like this. He hated surprises, that she knew for certain.

And he and Mama had always warned her not to go near the mine where he worked. Would he be angry she'd ridden all this way with one of his workers? Trusting Mr. Coulter had been a good choice, far better than trying to drive the wagon and care for the babe on her own.

What would Father think about Ruby? She honestly had no idea. She'd like to think he'd approve of her helping others.

She glanced down at the basket where Ruby slept. So peaceful at last. She'd woken an extra time to eat in the night, then had been fussy all morning. But about a quarter hour ago she finally gave in to sleep. If only Grace could do the same. So many weeks of interrupted nights left her perpetually weary.

Mr. Coulter nodded ahead. "There's the town."

Her heart picked up speed as she studied the cluster of buildings emerging from the barren landscape.

This was it. The moment of truth.

She tried to still her restless foot, but it seemed to have a mind of its own. She curled her fingers around the edge of the wagon seat, knuckles whitening.

Mr. Coulter must have sensed her unease, for he glanced over, his brow furrowed with concern. "Does your father have any idea you're coming?"

She shook her head, not trusting her voice to keep steady.

"You think he'll be upset you've come to find him?" There was a note of apprehension in his tone.

Grace swallowed hard. "No." But even to her own ears, the word sounded feeble and unconvincing. Weak. She couldn't let herself be weak. She had to show confidence.

Mr. Coulter's frown deepened. "When was the last time you saw him?"

"A little over a month ago."

He looked as though he wanted to say more, but they'd reached the first buildings on the outskirts of town.

She stared at all the unfamiliar shops and houses. So many. She only had one memory of seeing a town—Canvas Creek— but it hadn't been this big. Had it?

A river flowed behind the structures to the right, its waters dark and turbulent. A handful of men milled about the street, barely sparing a glance at their approaching wagon.

"Jedidiah's staying at the hotel." Mr. Coulter spoke quietly. "I'll take you there first and help you get settled. They should have a room available for you and the babe. Your things will be safe in the wagon at the livery, and I'll see to it the goat has a stall as well."

Grace nodded but couldn't speak. She tried to envision the reunion with her father. The speech she'd rehearsed over and over during the journey now seemed so inadequate. How would he react to her sudden appearance—and the baby? Anger? Shock? She couldn't picture any other response.

Would he open his arms and welcome her? Not likely. He'd hugged her when she was a girl—when he arrived for a visit and when he would leave. But that affection had ended many years ago.

They'd become polite to each other. When he came, he asked how she and her mother fared. The last time, after Mama passed, he'd not even dismounted his horse. She'd come outside to meet him, and he'd inquired about how she was getting along. When she told him how hard it was, how much she missed Mama, he hadn't responded at all. Maybe he'd not known what to say. Surely, he missed his wife too. He'd simply questioned whether Oren had come to deliver supplies that month, and when she said yes, he nodded. Then he'd turned and rode away.

As Mr. Coulter brought the wagon to a halt in front of the hotel, her heart pounded, and she couldn't catch a full breath. She clutched the handle of Ruby's basket.

He hopped down and came around to assist her. For a moment, she wanted nothing more than to cling to the safety of the wagon bench, to flee back to the lonely familiarity of the house in the valley.

Why did she ever think this was a good idea? She was doing this for her freedom. She just needed a little money from her father, then she could start anew somewhere else. Somewhere with people, where loneliness wouldn't consume her.

With Mama gone, she couldn't take the isolation. Not another day.

She finally placed her gloved hand in Mr. Coulter's, then used his strength for support as she stepped down from the wagon. She worked to ignore the warmth that spread up her cheeks as his fingers enveloped hers.

"Thank you," she managed to say.

"It's my pleasure." He smiled, but his eyes still held a glimpse of worry. Was his concern about her encounter with Father as well? "I'll get the basket."

She let him reach in and hoist Ruby in a smooth motion.

As he started to walk forward, she caught his sleeve. "Mr. Coulter?"

He paused, eyebrows arched.

"I...I wanted to thank you for bringing me here." She bit her bottom lip. She couldn't make herself meet his eyes. The air between them seemed charged with...she couldn't say what. Maybe only her nerves.

"I'm glad I was there to help." His voice came gentle, a lifeline. She finally met his gaze and let herself sink into those eyes. They understood. Somehow, they understood.

She took in a breath, filling her chest fully, then let out a long stream of worry.

"We'll get through this." The corners of his eyes crinkled. It wasn't a smile exactly, but it eased the weight on her chest.

She nodded. "Good."

Together, they took the two steps up to the hotel door, and he opened it to allow her entrance. The space inside somehow felt massive and small at the same time. The ceiling in this first area wasn't nearly as tall as their cabin in the valley. But the stairs ahead rose up and up. Greenery and red bows wrapped around the posts.

Christmas. She'd been trying not to remember the holiday. Mama had always made their home festive for that day. Without her here, there seemed no point in celebrating. And taking care of Ruby required all Grace's energy.

On her left stood a closed door, but the area on their right was open. An office of sorts. The man sitting at a desk looked up. Recognition lit his eyes and he stood. "Mr. Coulter. You're back."

Mr. Coulter nodded. "Yep. Do you have a room for Miss Hampton here?"

The clerk's face fell. "Sorry, we're all full up. The only room left is the one I held for you."

Mr. Coulter didn't hesitate. "Then give that room to Miss Hampton. I'll find another place to stay."

The clerk began to protest. "But sir—"

"It's fine. Please see that Miss Hampton is comfortable." Mr. Coulter's tone brooked no argument.

The man nodded and reached under the desk, producing a brass key. "Of course. Room one, top of the stairs and to your left, miss."

Grace accepted the key with a murmured thanks. She hated feeling like an unwanted complication in these men's lives. She followed Mr. Coulter up the narrow staircase, the wooden steps creaking under their feet.

At the top, he led her down the hall to the first door on the left, marked with a tarnished number one. "Your father is across the way in room two. I'm not sure if he's there now or not." He spoke in barely more than a whisper. "If not, we can go search for him when I'm back from the livery."

She nodded but didn't try to speak. Her tongue felt thick and heavy, her mouth dry as cotton.

He eased Ruby's basket down inside the room, then backed out. "I'll return shortly." He held her gaze for an extra beat, then turned and retreated down the hallway.

Something in his expression though…

She took in a long breath, then let it flow out. She wasn't alone in this. He'd helped so much already. And that parting look had said he wouldn't leave her until she was ready for him to.

She turned to take in the space that would be her lodging—a small, tidy room with a narrow cot, washstand, chest of drawers, and chair. She and Ruby could manage well here.

She moved to the bed and sank down on the edge. The mattress crinkled, far thinner than the down tick she used at home. What had they stuffed it with, paper?

She stared at the closed door, pulse thrumming in her ears. Only a few feet and two wooden doors separated her from her father. She'd traveled so many miles to get here, and yet she dreaded crossing that final threshold. Cowardice, plain and simple.

But Mr. Coulter had offered to help, so she could simply take him up on his offer and wait till he returned.

~

She'd run out of things to do.

Ruby still slept, and Grace had paced the room so many times she'd probably worn the last bit of finish off the wood floor. How long could it take to park the wagon and unharness the horses?

She walked to the window to look out at the street again. Maybe if she stared long enough, Mr. Coulter would appear.

She only had to stand there a moment before he stepped around the building on the end.

His broad shoulders filled the space as he strode down the street, his long legs eating up the distance with purposeful steps. The strength and confidence he exuded seemed to wrap around her like a warm blanket, promising protection and security.

When he disappeared from view under the awning, she turned to face the door, heart pounding as she waited for his knock.

The scuff of his boots on the stairs came first. He seemed to be trying to walk quietly, but that was no easy task. When the steps stopped, a soft knock sounded on the door.

She hurried over and pulled it open. "Mr. Coulter."

His gaze found hers, searching her face. Was he looking for signs of distress? "Is everything all right?"

"Yes." Did she sound too breathless? "I haven't seen my father yet."

She couldn't bring herself to say she'd been waiting for him. That made her sound helpless.

But understanding softened his expression. "Want me to knock on his door? See if he's in?"

"Please." Her voice pitched too high with the word.

He turned to the door across the hall and rapped against the wood, louder than he'd done on her door. His voice carried more strength too. "It's Sampson Coulter."

She stood in her own doorway and held her breath, straining for any sound of movement from within. Nothing came, but the door swung open a moment later, revealing her father's stern face. His gaze ignored Mr. Coulter, locking directly on her. He didn't look surprised. Had he heard her already?

She fought the urge to shrink back under the weight of his scrutiny, forcing herself to muster a smile. "Hello, Father." Her voice trembled a little. "I've come to find you."

Mr. Coulter took a small step back, clearing the space between her and her father. She waited for Father to step forward, to close the distance himself. But he remained planted in his doorway, his eyes never leaving her face. Was that anger? He was so hard to read. Why didn't he say anything?

Drawing in a breath, she took a tentative step forward.

Her father's jaw tightened, and she halted. The lines around his mouth deepened. "Why are you here, Grace?" The flatness in his tone made it impossible to gauge his mood. Was he angry? Annoyed?

She swallowed hard, scrambling for her rehearsed speech. "I...I can't stay at the house in the valley anymore. Not alone." The words tumbled out. "I'm going mad by myself. I need...I want to find a place in a town. I'll work, earn my keep. You won't have to worry with me anymore. I only need..."

Her throat closed up, choking off the rest. Even now, she couldn't bring herself to ask for money. To beg for his help.

"You need money," he finished flatly. Then his gaze cut to Mr. Coulter, sharpening. "And what exactly are you doing with my daughter? Why is she in your room?"

Mr. Coulter met her father's question with a calm steadiness she would love to possess. "I met Miss Hampton outside the mine yesterday. She needed to reach you, so I offered to bring her to you here. There aren't any other rooms available, so I gave her mine. I'll be sleeping at the livery. Nothing improper has happened. You have my word."

The suspicion in her father's eyes didn't waver. If anything, it intensified as he turned back to her. "So, you spent the night with my daughter, and now she's living with you."

A gasp slipped out before she could stop it, and heat surged up her neck. "No! It's not like that at all. Mr. Coulter helped me. He never..." She trailed off, the rest of her defense lodging in her throat as her father's cold stare silenced her.

How could he even think such a thing of her?

"Enough." Her father's voice snapped like a whip. He leveled a finger at Mr. Coulter. "You've compromised my daughter's virtue. There's only one way to remedy that. You'll marry her. Today."

The words struck like a physical blow, driving the air from her lungs. Marry a man she barely knew? The very idea was ludicrous. Impossible. And yet, her father looked determined.

Mr. Coulter didn't seem nearly as shocked as she felt. He just...studied him. He tipped his head, as though trying to see deeper. "And why would you want that, sir?"

He seemed to be asking more than the words implied, but she couldn't decipher what. Her stomach knotted tighter with each frantic beat of her pulse.

Her father spoke, each word sharp as a knife. "Because I want it. That should be reason enough."

A few beats later, Mr. Coulter dipped his chin. Then he turned to face her fully.

When his eyes met hers, they softened, warming with an emotion she dared not try to name. "Miss Hampton, I would be honored if you would agree to be my wife. I promise you'll never need for anything, and you can make your home anywhere you wish."

His tone was sincere, almost pleading. Did he want her to say yes? To go along with this insanity? Shouldn't he want to do whatever it took to get out of her father's demand?

But something in his steady blue gaze held her.

A steadiness. A calmness. Part of her yearned to lean into his strength, to take shelter in the security he offered. And yet, she resisted, bitterly chafing against her father making this decision for her.

He'd controlled every aspect of her life for so long. She couldn't let him take this choice from her too. Not when she'd finally gathered the courage to break free of him.

Tearing her gaze from Mr. Coulter's, she forced herself to face her father head on. "I need time to think about it." Her voice quavered but didn't break.

His eyes flashed, but he didn't say anything. Just took a step back and motioned for Mr. Coulter to enter his room. "We need to talk."

Mr. Coulter turned to give her a final look as he obeyed her father's command. His eyes appeared almost pleading. For her to say yes? That didn't make sense at all.

Why could he possibly want to be saddled with a wife? And a baby?

Backing into her room, she closed the door and leaned against it. What now? Did she agree to marry him? This stranger she'd only met yesterday? Though hadn't she already thought about how trustworthy he'd proven himself in that short time?

What was her other option?

To run away and figure out how to fend for herself. She wouldn't have the benefit of money to find a place to live before she looked for work. But surely, she could find something that offered both. Room and board as part of payment. Would she still be able to care for Ruby while she worked?

Mr. Coulter had said she could make her home wherever she chose. Had he meant that? If he would give her even a little money, or if by marrying him, her father would give her a little, she'd have a significant advantage in her new life on her own.

A memory surfaced, the one of him kneeling in front of Ruby the night before. Talking to her and letting her hold his finger. That sight had melted her heart. A man who would be that tender with a babe could surely be trusted to keep his word, couldn't he?

Maybe one had nothing to do with the other. But at least agreeing to her father's madness would buy her a little time. Time to figure out her next step.

CHAPTER 5

*D*read pooled in Sampson's gut as he stepped across the threshold, following Jedidiah's short, wiry frame into his hotel room.

Yet, he would have to talk to this man. Spend time with him. Willingly submit himself to whatever Jedidiah wanted to discuss or do.

No. Not *willingly*. That was never how it worked with this man.

No one disobeyed Jedidiah's orders without risking life or limb. Sampson couldn't put Miss Hampton's safety in jeopardy, even if she was the scoundrel's daughter. Nor could he break Jedidiah's trust, which he'd worked so hard to build. His family's mine and ranch depended on staying in this man's good graces.

He'd never thought the cost would be as high as marrying a woman he didn't even know and taking on a child that wasn't his—or hers, come to think of it. But he'd pay whatever price he had to pay to fix his mistakes.

Since he had no choice but to play along, he might as well find a pleasant expression.

A small part of him wondered if Jedidiah really thought he'd done something to compromise his daughter. Probably not. More likely, forcing the marriage simply suited the man's plans. He'd done far worse to get what he wanted.

And not once had Sampson seen even a hint of remorse on his face. Only a ruthless pursuit of his own interests.

The older man crossed to the window, casting his features into shadow as he turned back to Sampson. "Did you bring all the powder?"

Of course that would be his first concern. Not the daughter he apparently hadn't seen in some time. Sampson kept his voice steady. "It's safe in the wagon, stored at the livery."

Jedidiah's gaze narrowed. "We don't want to leave it there for long. It'd be a shame if it blew and wasted the whole supply."

Sampson only nodded, doing his best not to think of the kind livery owner who lived in a room in the back. And all those horses. And the goat Miss Hampton needed for little Ruby's food.

"We should be ready to set out in a couple days." Jedidiah's voice cut through his thoughts. The older man fixed him with a penetrating stare. "That will give you time to get your new wife settled so we can focus on work."

Again, Sampson could only nod. Clearly, he had no choice but to go through with the marriage. At least he could make sure Miss Hampton and Ruby got to a place safe from all this trouble. "Do you want to be there for the ceremony?"

A glint of something akin to amusement flashed in Jedidiah's eyes. "Of course. It's my right to give my only daughter away." His bushy gray brows rose. "I only hope you'll be the husband she deserves."

Sampson clenched his jaw, forcing a grin to play along. "I'll do my best by her."

"We'll see about that." Jedidiah turned back to the window. "Go on now. Find that deputy for the vows. I'll be along soon enough."

"Yes, sir." He slipped from the room, careful not to show how badly he wanted to get away from the man.

In the hallway, he paused outside Miss Hampton's door. He needed to speak with her. He'd rather not have her father listening in, though. He was pretty sure the man must have heard them talking earlier, which was why he'd not been surprised at the sight of his daughter.

Sampson kept his knock quiet, and the door swung open a moment later. Miss Hampton's wide gaze met his, then dropped to the babe she was feeding.

Ruby nestled in one of her arms, eyes closed as she drank from the bottle. So tiny. So innocent. That urge to protect them both crept through him once more.

He lifted his focus to Miss Hampton. Were her eyes rimmed in red? She'd been crying, probably because of this marriage her father was forcing on her.

The weight on his chest pressed a little harder. He was part of this debacle that brought her pain. He couldn't stop it, but he could do his best to help her see this would be a benefit for her and Ruby.

He kept his voice quiet. "Would you like to go downstairs?" He nodded over his shoulder toward Jedidiah's door across the hall.

Seeming to understand his meaning, she nodded and stepped out of her room. He followed her down the stairs, and when they reached the foyer, she turned to him.

He raised his brows. "Are you hungry? There's a cafe down the street." She hadn't brought her coat. Ruby would need a warmer blanket too. "I can run up and grab your wrap, and maybe a heavier cover for Ruby."

She shook her head. "I'm not hungry." Her expression looked miserable.

He motioned to the parlor across from the clerk's desk. The closed door would give them some privacy.

She followed him inside.

After closing the door, he motioned to the sofa. "Do you want to sit?" Ruby might be getting heavy in her arms.

But she shook her head, facing him again. She took a deep breath and met his gaze squarely. "Upstairs, you asked me to marry you. You did that because my father insisted, but I need you to know, you don't have to go along with it. I don't need anything from him. Or you. Ruby and I can just leave. Set out on our own."

He inhaled. At least she hadn't outright refused. She was probably just trying to give him the option to take it back.

He didn't need that, and he wouldn't take it either. How could he explain?

Lord, give me the right words.

How much did she know about her father? It seemed almost impossible to believe she wouldn't be aware of the kind of man he was. Yet, Miss Hampton had an innocence, a gentleness that made him think she might be naïve to the extent of her father's crimes.

He might as well ask. "How well do you know your father?"

Her brows pulled together, and she glanced back toward the stairs. Was she worried about Jedidiah overhearing? Or did she think Sampson might tell him what she said?

She returned her gaze to Sampson. "He runs a mining business. It's a lot of work and can be dangerous. He came to visit Mama and me every month."

So, not often enough to truly know the ugly side of the man. Jedidiah showed only what he wanted others to see. "Did you ever live with him?"

She shook her head. "Mama and I always lived in our house in the valley while he lived at the mine."

The babe reached the end of the milk in her bottle, and Grace pulled it away. She shifted Ruby up to her shoulder and rubbed her back.

He reached for the bottle to free her hands.

"Thank you." Miss Hampton murmured the words as she focused on the babe.

Ruby opened one eye as she lay against Miss Hampton, and her brown hair stuck out in several directions. That adorable innocent expression… Something warm tightened in his chest. He'd never thought a tiny baby could be so cute. So… He didn't have words to express how much she'd taken hold of him.

If he and Miss Hampton married, he would be Ruby's father. The thought struck like a bolt of lightning.

He wouldn't really be, though. He had offered her a marriage with no strings. She could be on her own, safe and provided for. He would never try to control her like her father did.

And on that point, how much should he tell her about her father? It seemed cruel to dash the image she carried of him. But she needed to know why it was important to go along with Jedidiah's wishes if they could make it work.

Lord, give me wisdom.

He took a breath. "I've worked for your father a few months now."

She looked up from Ruby, though she kept patting the babe's back. Her gaze held his, but she didn't speak.

"Your father has a lot of power in McPharland's business. McPharland doesn't care much about how things get done as long as they do. Your father uses whatever means necessary to make sure that happens. He doesn't think twice about having men beaten or even killed to make sure things go his way."

Her face paled, and she swayed slightly.

Had he said too much? He reached out to steady her, but she shook her head. "I'm fine. I'm not that delicate."

Wasn't she, though?

He dropped his hand, and when she lifted her chin a little, he dared go on. "I'd feel better if you and Ruby weren't at the mercy of your father. I'd rather give you my name and make sure you have a nice place to live—a safe place. I'll make sure you want for nothing." She studied him with furrowed brow. He let his eyes plead with her as he said this last part. "Please consider it. For Ruby's sake, if nothing else."

Her expression didn't change, she simply...stared at him. What thoughts churned in that mind of hers? Did she believe him?

Or did she think he was on her father's side, trying to manipulate her into giving him control?

Show her the truth, Lord.

At last, her mouth parted as she prepared to speak. Her voice came out hesitant. "Would you expect to...live with us? Like a real husband?"

He shook his head, fighting off the burn in his cheeks at what she really asked. "You can live wherever you like. My family has a ranch a day's ride from here. You're welcome to move in there. Or if you want to be on your own, near a town, we'll find a place you like." He forced himself to meet her gaze again. They had to be honest with each, and he couldn't let embarrassment get in the way of anything she needed to ask. "I won't expect anything from you. Nothing like in a usual marriage."

Her shoulders sagged a little, as if in relief. But a small furrow remained between her brows. "Why are you doing this? Why would you willingly burden yourself with us?"

He let himself consider her question. Why *did* he want her to say yes so much? He didn't owe her anything. She was the daughter of his enemy—kin to the man who stole a year's worth of sapphires from his family.

But this woman was different. Nothing like Jedidiah. And for some reason, he craved to keep her safe. To protect her from the evil who'd sired her. She didn't deserve to be at that man's mercy. Nor did the sweet child.

Sampson could help her *so* easily. Not only did he have

money from his share of the sapphires, which he'd saved for years, he also had his pay from McPharland.

He swallowed as he tried to put all this into words. "I can help you." His voice graveled with how much he wanted to do that. And then he let himself say the real truth. "And maybe in helping you, I can make up for my own mistakes."

Seconds stretched as she searched his face. Something in her eyes seemed to say she understood him. Maybe too much.

At last, she gave a slow nod. "All right. I'll marry you, Mr. Coulter." Her arms tightened around Ruby. "To keep her safe, I'll do whatever I have to."

Relief washed through him, though it was tempered by the knowledge of what lay ahead. Marrying her was the easy part. Figuring out how to extricate her and Ruby from her father's clutches and put an end to the man's crimes for good—that would be far more difficult. And exceedingly dangerous.

One step at a time. He had to secure her safety first. The rest would come.

He allowed a smile. "I'm glad." Then he tipped his head toward the door. "I'll go find the deputy and see if he can meet us here in an hour. Is that enough time for you to get ready?"

She nodded. "I don't need long." Of course she didn't. She'd not had weeks to plan an elaborate ceremony. This was probably nothing like the wedding a young woman might dream of. His chest squeezed at the thought how disappointed she must be.

He reached for the door but paused, looking back to meet her eyes once more. "It will be all right, Miss Hampton. I promise."

Her lips trembled, but after a moment, she nodded. "Thank you, Mr. Coulter. Truly."

The earnestness in her voice, despite the circumstances, undid him. He struggled to clear the tightness in his throat.

"You're welcome to call me Sampson." His brothers called him Sam sometimes, but he'd never liked that nickname.

The shadows in her eyes eased a little. "You can call me Grace."

Grace. He let his mouth shape the word. "I like that name. It suits you." Her beauty outshone any sapphire, that was for certain.

He allowed himself a final look at the woman and child who would soon be his family. He would be a lucky man, even if the marriage didn't come in the usual way or with the typical advantages.

Then he slipped out. Time to set the next step in motion.

The sooner they wed, the sooner he could spirit her and Ruby away from here. To safety.

CHAPTER 6

$\mathcal{W}$hat would Sampson think of her? Nervous energy hummed through Grace's entire body.

She tucked the last pin into place and gave her hair one more pat. The braid coiled around her head would have to do. She couldn't create the fancy styles Mama had been able to, but with a ribbon woven through the braid, this looked pretty enough. Didn't it? Hopefully Sampson would agree.

Not that he'd agreed to a real marriage. Even so, for some reason, she wanted him to be pleased with her appearance as his bride.

It was silly to worry so. She pivoted from the mirror.

Ruby had played quietly while she worked, an accomplishment in itself.

She smiled down at the little one lying on the bed and gripping the leather strip she loved. "We're going to get married today, Ruby."

The babe's blue eyes blinked at her as she cooed like she understood every word.

Grace held in a sigh. "I hope so. I hope I'm doing the right thing." She had to stop questioning herself. She'd made the decision, and the time had come to carry it out.

She scooped up Ruby and grabbed the basket so she would have a place to lay her during the ceremony. A scan around the room showed nothing else she needed. Was she missing something?

Most women had weeks or months to prepare for a wedding. If only Mama were here. She turned toward the door to ward off the grief that would overwhelm her if she let it. She had to focus on getting through this next hour. Nothing else.

She descended the stairs with Ruby in one arm and the basket swinging from the other.

Her father waited at the bottom. His dark gaze honed on her, bringing the realization that he didn't know about Ruby yet.

She forced a pleasant expression, as much as she wanted to cower.

When she reached the bottom step, he demanded, "Whose child is that?"

Grace met his piercing eyes, her heart pounding. "This is Ruby. She's... I've taken her in as my ward. As my daughter."

His eyes narrowed. "Your daughter? What nonsense is this?"

"Her mother died, and her father left her in my care." She glanced at the open parlor door. "It's a long story, and one we don't have time for now."

It took some courage to step away from him and move toward the room.

Thankfully, her father didn't try to stop her.

Sampson stood near the hearth, another man at his side. Sampson's gaze locked on her as she entered, his brown eyes soft. He stepped forward, holding something green.

She met him partway, and he took the basket from her and extended a holly branch. He gave her a sheepish smile. "I thought you might like something pretty to hold, even though it's not the season for flowers."

Warmth soaked through her at the thoughtful gesture. He'd somehow found a moment, amidst all the arrangements and bringing her bags from the livery to consider what she might want. She accepted the gift, her fingers brushing his. Tingles crept up her arm from the contact, but she did her best to ignore them. "It's perfect. Thank you."

And it was. The shiny green leaves and bright red berries added a festive touch to the simple ceremony.

She met his gaze and sank into the warmth there, the sincerity. He was truly trying to make this special for her, even in the midst of the chaos. Her chest tightened with unexpected emotion.

The deputy cleared his throat. "Are we ready to begin?"

Grace nodded, not trusting her voice. She settled Ruby in her basket, then straightened and moved to stand with Sampson in front of the deputy.

Someone had brought in a few extra candles to place on the mantel, and their glow lit the space as the deputy began the simple ceremony.

He read the vows, and she managed to speak her parts in a clear, mostly-steady voice.

It felt surreal to be pledging herself to a man she barely knew. Yet something about his solid, reassuring presence beside her and the care he'd already shown made it seem right. If she had to enter a hasty marriage, there was no one she'd rather bind herself to than this man who'd already proven himself countless times in two short days.

"I now pronounce you man and wife." The deputy closed the book in his hand. "Mr. and Mrs. Sampson Coulter."

Mrs. Sampson Coulter.

The name echoed in her mind as the weight of it settled on

her. She was no longer a Hampton, but a Coulter. Bound to this man and his family she had yet to meet.

She wasn't sure exactly how to feel about the change. But she couldn't go back now.

Sampson's warm hand settled at the small of her back. She hated to pull away to gather Ruby, and he saved her the trouble as he reached for the basket, then resettled himself at Grace's side. "Shall we go upstairs?"

Before she could answer, her father's sharp voice cut through the room. "Coulter. A word."

Sampson paused, and when he spoke, his voice came out measured. "Can it wait? I'd like to see my wife and...daughter settled first."

The word *daughter* brought a flutter to Grace's stomach. Never mind that he'd just called her wife. This would take so much getting used to.

Her father's eyes flashed. "We've work to do."

The challenge in his expression couldn't be denied. He was testing Sampson's loyalty. This wasn't a battle worth fighting, not when they needed to keep him appeased.

She touched Sampson's arm. "It's all right. I'm going to put Ruby down for a nap anyway. You do what you need to."

Uncertainty flicked in his eyes as he searched her face. She tried to convey without words that she understood, that she knew he was doing his best to take care of her.

After a long moment, he nodded and spoke softly. "I'll be up soon. And I'll make sure to keep quiet so I don't wake Ruby."

She gave him a small smile of gratitude before taking the babe in her basket. As she left the men behind and climbed the stairs, a part of her appreciated the solitude. She needed a chance to absorb all that had happened in the last hour. To fully comprehend that she had become a married woman.

But as she entered their room and shut the door behind her,

a wave of loneliness spread through her. The space felt too big, too empty without Sampson's steadying presence.

She couldn't let herself grow accustomed to relying on him. In the end, it would always be only her and Ruby. Like it had been her and Mama, together but alone.

Sampson might be her husband in name, but she knew all too well what that meant—provide financially, and nothing else. Not companionship. Certainly not love.

Her own father had been nothing more than a peripheral figure, flitting in and out of their lives as he pleased. She couldn't let herself be disappointed when Sampson did the same.

With a sigh, she settled Ruby in the center of the bed, stroking a hand over the baby's dark downy hair. "Looks like it's just you and me, sweet girl."

Ruby cooed in response, blinking up at her with those innocent blue eyes. So trusting.

Together, they would be fine. She could be content. Happy even. And she would make sure Ruby never wanted for love.

~

*S*ampson's bones ached from the bitter cold as he rode the bay lead gelding down the rocky slope in the darkness. The chestnut maneuvered beside them, with the pair still hitched together.

He'd delivered the blasting powder to the location Jedidiah specified, several hours west of Missoula. The man had wanted the powder left in the wagon, so any horses could be hitched to move it if the need arose. Which meant Sampson rode the team back instead of driving them. The sun had long since set, and it would be well after midnight before he reached Missoula Mills.

And Grace. His wife.

The thought of her spurred him onward, despite the exhaustion that dragged at him. He couldn't shake the feeling that something was wrong, that Jedidiah had ulterior motives for sending him off so abruptly after the wedding. The man was as cunning as a fox and a thousand times more ruthless.

Would he try to take Ruby away? Force Grace to leave with him? Sampson had to get back to them, had to make sure they were safe.

At least the location Jedidiah had ordered Sampson to take the blasting powder was in the opposite direction from the Coulter ranch. Sampson had been pretty sure this project didn't involve his family, and the location he'd been sent to tonight was one more confirmation.

Jedidiah had said something about wanting to prepare for a new mine up in these mountains, though he hadn't given any details. And Sampson knew better than to ask questions.

If only he had it in him to shoot both Mick and Jedidiah outright. That had been his original plan when he first went after Mick McPharland—to make the man pay for what he'd done to Sampson's family. For stealing a wagonload of sapphires and burning down his brother Jonah's cabin.

But he'd not had the nerve to pull the trigger. Mick always had too many people around, and shooting from a distance like a hired gun...well, he couldn't quite make himself take a human life in cold blood.

So he'd signed on to work for McPharland. He'd figured he'd learn more about the operation and find a weakness. A way to bring the man down. He'd quickly realized Jedidiah's mean streak ran even deeper than McPharland's.

And time after time, no matter how much he tried to work himself up into righteous anger, thinking of all the people who had been robbed or hurt or killed at the hands of these blackguards, he still couldn't bring himself to pull the trigger.

All he could do was stay close. Do everything possible to

make sure they trusted him. That way, he'd know if they targeted his family's ranch again.

He'd find out in time to stop them or warn his brothers.

He should use this time to come up with a solid plan for how exactly he would pull that off.

So far, the only idea he'd been able to think of was telling Jedidiah the Coulters' sapphire mine had run dry, but that they'd found another bunch of gems on land beyond theirs, and they just hadn't had the chance to stake a claim yet. That last part was actually true. Or rather, Two Stones had found sapphires on land that neighbored the Coulters'. He'd brought them the stones and said they were welcome to mine it if they wished. That had been a few weeks before he left, and none of his brothers had been in a hurry to claim it. They had plenty to handle with their own still-productive mine and ranch.

Hopefully Jedidiah would go after the new claim and leave his family's property alone.

It wouldn't be enough, though. If he convinced Jedidiah, and his men started mining the new area, it would keep Jedidiah and Mick too close. He had to come up with something better. Some way to get the men to leave the area completely.

The harsh clop of the horses' hooves against the frozen ground echoed in the night air. The biting wind nipped at his exposed skin, but he barely noticed, too consumed by the gnawing worry that twisted in his gut.

He reached the livery at nearly one in the morning. His body ached as he dismounted and handed the team off to a bleary-eyed McDonough.

Then he jogged down the dimly-lit street toward the hotel. When he slipped into the building, he tried to keep his boot-steps quiet on the stairs, but his heart hammered with urgency.

After easing open the door to their room, he peered inside. All was dark and quiet. Were Grace and Ruby here?

He stepped in, walking toe-first to be soundless—a skill Two

Stones had taught all the Coulter boys as they hunted in the woods around the ranch.

The barely audible hum of breathing pricked his ears as he closed the door behind him. He crept closer to the bed and finally made out Grace's slender form under the quilts. Moonlight from the window fell over the top of her head, revealing the creamy skin of her brow and loose tendrils of her hair fanning over the cover.

So beautiful.

The urge to reach out and stroke her cheek struck him with an almost irresistible force, but he held himself back. He'd made a promise to let her be free, and he'd not betray her trust with even the smallest of liberties.

He'd never given much thought to marriage. Women weren't plentiful in this Montana wilderness, especially not the kind he'd choose.

And yet, by some miracle, this woman had become his *wife*. The word felt foreign on his tongue, the weight of it both terrifying and exhilarating.

She was a treasure, one he'd love to cherish and protect, not merely support from afar. If he could just break free from Jedidiah's iron grip, perhaps she would allow him to stay close.

He let himself imagine it for a moment—a life with them, not as husband and wife, but simply as a family. He would never force Grace into physical closeness, not that he'd shy away if she were willing. But simply to be near her and sweet Ruby, to watch over them and ensure no harm came—he could be content with that. Surely. It would be a far sight better than stopping in with supplies once a month.

But first, he had to find a way to stop Jedidiah and Mick for good.

He stepped around the bed to peer into Ruby's basket, but thick shadows kept him from making out the details of her small form. Her steady breathing sounded normal, so he eased back. Best he roll out his blankets and bed down on the floor.

Tomorrow, he would figure out where his wife and daughter would be safest and get things started to settle them there—far away from Jedidiah. To accomplish that feat, he'd need every bit of strategy he could muster.

CHAPTER 7

*T*he babe's cry tugged at Grace, but her body clung desperately to sleep.

Another cry.

She had to get up. Ruby needed to eat. Grace cracked open her eyes, the lids so heavy she could hardly lift them. She'd never imagined how exhausting it would be taking care of a baby. Especially every night.

Ruby called out again, this wail more urgent.

Yes, little one. I know you're hungry.

Grace dragged herself upright, shoulders sagging under the weight of exhaustion. Her mind felt muddled, thoughts sluggish as she tried to remember...

Sampson.

Had he returned last night? She glanced around the small room. His bedroll still lay against the wall. Was it in the same position? Yes...maybe.

Worry stirred in her middle. Her father had sent him out of town on an errand. Had he run into trouble?

Ruby's insistent sobs drew her back to her primary concern.

With effort, she swung her legs over the side of the bed and leaned down to the basket, swaying a little as a wave of dizziness washed over her. Ruby fussed, her face scrunched and red.

"Shh, I'm here," Grace cooed, reaching in to lift the squirming bundle into her arms.

Ruby's cries quieted to whimpers as she nuzzled against Grace's neck, rooting for milk.

A soft knock at the door made Grace's insides tighten. Her father? The thought made her heart pound.

But then a familiar deep voice called through the wood. "Grace? It's Sampson. Can I come in?"

Her pulse shifted to a different kind of racing. Not fear this time but…nerves. She let out a shaky breath. "Yes."

The door creaked open, revealing Sampson's broad frame. In his hands, he carried a steaming mug and a plate laden with food. "I thought you might be ready for some breakfast." His voice came low, not loud enough to carry through the wall to her father's room.

When his warm brown eyes met hers, they softened and roamed her face. Ruby made another fussing sound, and his gaze dropped to the babe. "Is she hungry?"

She nodded, turning her focus to her highest priority. She reached for the bottle she'd readied after the last time Ruby woke. "I'll need to feed her before I can eat. Thank you for bringing the meal though. And coffee." The rich aroma filled the room, giving her a tiny bit of clarity with only the scent of it.

Sampson stepped closer, moving around Ruby's basket to set the food and drink on the small table beside the bed. This space felt so much smaller with his presence filling it. "I could... Would you like me to try to feed her? While you eat?"

Surprise flashed through her. Other than that first night in the trapper's cabin when he'd knelt to talk to Ruby, Sampson had kept a respectful distance, letting Grace be the one to tend to the baby's needs. He'd never even held her.

But, if he was offering... He did look sincere, though a little nervous.

He always held such a confident air. Not arrogant or prideful, just...comfortable in his own skin. But the hesitation in his eyes, the way he held his upper body back a little, made her almost want to chuckle. If he could handle her father, then he was more than capable of feeding Ruby.

She gave a thankful smile. "If you don't mind, that would be wonderful."

She motioned for him to sit on the bed beside her, and he moved around to ease down where she'd pointed. He left nearly an arm's length between them, which meant she had to stand to step closer to place Ruby into his arms.

As the babe's weight settled on him, he seemed to go rigid. Not even breathing.

"Just relax with her." She placed the bottle in the babe's mouth, and Ruby latched on hungrily. "There's a girl. That's what you needed, isn't it?"

Sampson hadn't moved, still holding the babe with both arms so he didn't have a free hand to take the bottle.

Grace glanced up to see his expression. She'd not realized how close she stood, their faces only a handsbreadth apart.

His eyes were locked on Ruby, though, wonder transforming his rugged features. The rough edges softened, and a smile curved his lips as he watched the tiny girl drink from the bottle Grace held.

"She's so small." His voice came out in a rough whisper, like speaking louder would break the spell. "I've never held a baby before."

Her heart squeezed as warmth melted her insides. This strong, capable man cradled Ruby with such gentleness. Such awe. "You're doing great. You can let her legs rest on yours so you have a free hand to hold the bottle."

With an anxious grimace, he did as she said, easing his hand out from beneath the babe with painstaking care. Once he'd accomplished it, he let out an audible breath, and Grace bit back a smile. No need to worry about him being too rough with the child.

He took the bottle, their hands brushing in the transfer, and Grace fought her body's reaction as she stepped back. She eased out her own breath. Being so near him had her insides befuddled. How could he affect her so much?

She let herself stand and watch them. The big man—so handsome that he made her breath catch every time she looked at him—holding Ruby like the treasure she was.

Tears stung her eyes. She needed sleep or else she'd turn into a sappy mess. Ruby had been fussy until about midnight, then finally settled. But too many restless nights in a row had taken their toll. Grace would need more than a few unbroken hours of sleep to ever feel rested again.

Sampson lifted his gaze then, taking her in. "You're exhausted. Sit. Eat. I've got her."

Heat slipped up her neck at being caught staring, and she sat on the bed against the headboard, tucking her feet up under her nightdress. She needed to dress for the day, but she couldn't do that with Sampson here. Maybe she should be more concerned about him seeing her in sleeping attire, but she was too exhausted to waste energy on what she couldn't help.

Besides, he was her husband.

That thought brought a fresh wave of heat, and she reached for the plate and mug. The scent of fried eggs and ham made her stomach rumble, but she needed coffee first. She took a sip, and the warm liquid eased through her. Her eyes drifted closed as she relished the feeling. Was anything ever so wonderful as hot coffee on a cold morning?

When she opened her eyes again, Sampson was watching her, an unreadable expression on his face. He glanced down quickly, returning his focus to Ruby. The babe had already almost finished the bottle, her little mouth working more slowly now as sleep tugged at her.

Grace set the mug aside and picked up a piece of bread, tearing off a small bit to pop into her mouth. The fresh yeasty flavor burst on her tongue, and her stomach growled again, reminding her how ravenous she truly was.

As she ate, her gaze kept drifting to Sampson and Ruby. He'd relaxed into the task, his easy confidence fully returned. Grace's chest squeezed, a painful hope swelling beneath her ribs. If Sampson fell in love with Ruby, maybe he'd want to stay with them.

Stop it, she chided herself. Wishing for impossible things would only lead to heartache. Sampson had married her out of obligation, to keep her safe. Not for love.

She shook the thoughts away and focused on her food, working through the eggs and ham.

Soon, Ruby sucked the last of the milk. Sampson eased the bottle out of her mouth and set it aside, then shifted the baby up to rest against his shoulder. He threw Grace a hesitant glance. "Is this right? She needs to be burped?"

"Yes, just pat her back gently." He'd been watching. Paying attention. "You're doing wonderfully with her."

Color tinged his cheeks, and he ducked his head, focusing on Ruby as he patted her back with so much tenderness. After a moment, a tiny burp escaped the baby, and Sampson's face split into a grin, his eyes crinkling at the corners.

"There's a good girl." He changed his motion to rub circles on Ruby's back.

The babe gave a contented sigh, her eyes drifting closed as she snuggled against his broad shoulder.

You're a lucky girl, Ruby. Grace swallowed past the lump in her throat. She needed to shore up her defenses against this man's tenderness. "Did you find another place to sleep last night? I didn't hear you come in."

Sampson looked up, his brows lowered in confusion. "No, I slept here. On the floor." He nodded toward his bedroll, still tucked against the wall. "I got in late from your father's errand and didn't want to disturb you. Then I woke early to milk the goat." He gestured to the floor beside Ruby's basket.

For the first time, Grace noticed the jars of fresh milk lined up beside the wicker. Her heart squeezed, gratitude and something warmer, more tender, welling up inside her. She blinked back another rush of tears. "Thank you, Sampson. Truly."

It had been so long since she'd had anyone to rely on. Anyone who cared enough to lighten her burdens. And now Sampson, this man she barely knew, stepped in without hesitation.

He looked away, color deepening in his cheeks. "It's nothing. I'm happy to help how ever I can."

Ruby slept soundly against his chest, her petite lips parted and dark lashes fanning her round cheeks.

Sampson cleared his throat, drawing Grace's attention back to his face. He sobered, his brow furrowing as he met her gaze. "I guess we should talk about what you want to do next. Have you given any thought to where you'd like to settle?"

Her chest tightened, and she looked down at her hands where she clenched the plate. In truth, she'd been so focused on finding her father and keeping Ruby safe and cared for that she hadn't let herself make decisions about where to go once she had the funds to. "I guess I need to find a house somewhere."

He was quiet a moment. "You know, my family has a ranch. About a day's ride from here, nestled up on a mountain. It's a beautiful place. Really peaceful. And there's plenty of room. I have five brothers, and a few of them are married." He paused, as if gauging her reaction.

He'd mentioned the ranch before, but surely he didn't want her to go there and burden them.

His eyes softened. "You and Ruby, you'd be welcome there. They'd love to have you."

Her heart stuttered. His expression was earnest, sincere. A tiny flicker of hope sparked to life in her chest.

A real home. A place to belong. She tried to picture it—a sprawling ranch, the mountains rising in the distance, wildflowers dotting the meadows.

But she was a stranger to them. A woman who was imposing on their brother. Why would they want her to barge in? Especially with a baby. "Your family...they wouldn't mind? Having a strange woman and baby they don't know living with them?"

Sampson's eyes crinkled at the corners, a hint of a smile playing about his mouth. "Mind? They'd be over the moon. My sisters-in-law would dote on Ruby something fierce. Dinah, my oldest brother's wife, is a doctor, so she could help with anything the baby needs. And her sister has two little ones herself." He nodded toward Ruby. "Mary Ellen is only a couple years old, so these two could have fun together in time."

He shifted the baby, and she made a soft snuffling sound, nestling closer to his neck. The sight made Grace's heart clench with a fierce, protective longing. Sampson's family sounded wonderful. Warm and welcoming and everything she'd never had.

But so many people. So many eyes watching her, judging her. What if they found her lacking? What if they decided she wasn't good enough? Especially to be a mother. What if they decided Ruby would be better off without her? The thought made her throat close up and tears burn.

She swallowed hard, forcing the words past the tightness in her throat. "It sounds wonderful. Truly. But I think...maybe I'd rather settle with just Ruby and me for now. Until I find my feet." She tried for a smile, but it felt wobbly. "I don't want to impose on your family."

Concern etched in the lines of Sampson's face. He opened

his mouth as if to protest, then closed it again, giving a slow nod.

After a moment, he spoke, though his brow held a frown. "I understand wanting your independence. Missoula Mills is likely closest to where I'll be, but it's still a rough town. Nearly all the occupants are men—miners and trappers and such. I wouldn't feel comfortable leaving you and Ruby here alone."

She bit her lip. "What about Canvas Creek? I haven't been there since I was a girl, but I remember it being small."

He still looked troubled, his jaw tight as his focus moved out the window. "I'll make some inquiries, see what I can find out about available houses." He let out a sigh. "In the meantime, I've made arrangements with the cafe and the mercantile. You can purchase whatever you and Ruby need, and they'll put it on my account."

Grace stared at him, her middle giving a funny little flip. He'd thought of everything. "Thank you." But she wouldn't spend any of his money if she didn't have to. He was already doing so much.

As though he could hear her thoughts, he locked his gaze onto hers. Those deep brown eyes grew intense. "Grace, I mean it. If you or Ruby, or even the goat, have need of anything— clothes, food, a pretty bauble—please get it. If there's something you can't find in town, just let me know. I have a friend named Two Stones who's really good at locating hard-to-find goods in the area. He has connections all over the territory."

Warmth blossomed in her chest, spreading through her limbs like honey. The way he looked at her, the insistence in his voice, it made her feel…cared for. Cherished, even.

She managed a wobbly smile. "Thank you, Sampson. Truly. I don't know how I can ever repay your kindness."

He shook his head. "You don't need to repay me. I made a vow to care for you and Ruby, and I intend to keep it."

His words settled over her like a warm blanket, easing the

tension from her shoulders. She needed to find a distraction before the tears broke through her defenses. She worked for a smile. "Two Stones? That's an unusual name."

A soft smile curved his mouth. "He's Salish. And my family's closest friend. When we first moved to the Montana Territory, I was seven. Us boys were helping Dat build the cabin, and Two Stones showed up one day to help. He was the same age as my oldest brother, Jericho. He came back the next day. Then the next, and every day after until the house and barn were both built." Sampson's mouth rose in a grin.

"After that, he taught us how to hunt and survive in the mountains. In return, Dat taught him about God. Two Stones and his parents all came to faith, and he's been a good friend ever since. His village is about two hours' ride from our place, but he spends a fair amount of time on the trail. He married last year, and Heidi often rides with him."

Grace's mind scrambled to keep up with all the details. She'd never met any natives. Just seen a few who rode through their valley, but only from a distance.

One other comment from the flurry of words stuck in her mind. *Dat taught him about God.* Mama had shared the beliefs that some people held about an Almighty Being who created the world and all people. Mama said she never saw reason to believe it was true.

Did Sampson believe? Would it anger him if she asked? He'd not shown a temper with anything else, so maybe he wouldn't mind.

"You're a..." She struggled to find the right words. "I mean... you believe in...God?"

He tipped his head as he studied her. "I do. Does that mean you...don't?" He hesitated on that last word.

Would it be awful if she told him the truth? Would he not want to be married to her? Not want to help her and Ruby get settled in their own home?

She forced down the rising panic. She had no reason to think Sampson would do that. He didn't look angry. Only curious.

She searched for the best way to answer. "I don't know very much about Him." Was God a *Him*, or an *It*? Either way, this proved the truth of her statement. She pressed on. "My mother told me that some people believe in a God who made the world. That they believe they'll be carried to live with Him after they die." She hadn't actually said she didn't believe that, but her wording probably made it clear.

Sampson tipped his head a little, but then nodded. "I guess that's the basics of it, but there's a lot more. God *did* make us. He created the world and all the plants and animals thousands of years ago. But He didn't just make everything and walk away. He wants friendship with us. He wants us to know Him. To talk with Him. To feel how much He loves us."

She frowned as she let those ideas sink in. "How do you talk to God? Can you see Him?"

He shook his head. "Not like I see you. But you can talk out loud or just in your thoughts. He hears." Sampson hesitated as if he was trying to find the words. "It's hard to explain how you can tell, but...it's like I feel a peace when I talk to Him. Like I know my thoughts or words were heard."

He gave his head another little shake. "Anyway. I'm not the best one to explain it. Jericho or Jude would be better."

Something like sadness tinged his eyes. Was he disappointed she'd said no to staying with his family? That she likely wouldn't ever meet those two brothers?

Part of her wanted to take back that decision, if only to please Sampson. But she had to stick with her plans. She couldn't get used to relying on a man.

Maybe better to change the subject. She dropped her focus to Ruby. "I should get her changed so she can take a proper nap." She reached for the baby, and Sampson eased her into Grace's arms. His large hands brushed Grace's skin, raising gooseflesh up her arm.

He stood, his broad frame once more filling the small room. He hesitated, his gaze lingering on the baby. "I should start work. Your father will be wondering where I am." His voice was low, tinged with reluctance.

Grace nodded. "Thank you again, for everything."

He reached out, his fingertips grazing Ruby's downy cheek with a tenderness that made Grace's heart ache. Then, with a last, unreadable look, he turned and strode from the room, his boots thumping on the wooden floorboards.

As she listened to his retreating footsteps, a sense of loss settled in her chest. She pushed it away, turning her attention to the task at hand. She had much to do to get ready for their new life.

CHAPTER 8

*W*hat was Jedidiah up to now?

A chill bit into Sampson as he sat on the wagon bench outside the livery, his body turning stiff from the late afternoon cold as the sun sank lower in the sky. His boss had said to hitch the team and saddle his mount, and he'd meet Sampson here.

He'd had Sampson working all day, loading this rented wagon high with crates, then checking in with some of the businesses around town to find men who might be looking for work.

That meant Sampson had only seen Grace and Ruby once in passing. He'd hoped for a nice quiet evening with them, but whatever excursion Jedidiah had planned now probably meant they wouldn't be back until late again.

He couldn't shake the notion that something was going to change very soon. Jedidiah's secrecy was nothing new, but the sheer amount of supplies Sampson had loaded up suggested they were close to setting Jedidiah's plan into action.

What plan, though? What was he attempting to do?

Should Sampson try to get Grace settled in a house before

then? He had a feeling Jedidiah wouldn't allow him the time. For now, he'd spoken to Frank at the hotel and paid ahead for the room for two weeks. He'd also been careful to make sure Frank —and the café and the mercantile and McDonough here at the livery—knew Grace was Mrs. Coulter now, and that she should be given all the respect and protection his family name provided.

Should he speak to anyone else?

The thump of boots on frozen ground jerked him from his thoughts.

Jedidiah was striding toward him, a satisfied smirk on his weathered face. "Ready to ride out, boy?" Jedidiah didn't wait for an answer as he jerked his horse's rein untied, then swung up into the saddle.

Boy.

Sampson didn't react to the patronizing moniker, just released the wagon brake and gathered the reins. He signaled them forward behind his boss.

Jedidiah started out toward the east, not west like he'd sent Sampson last night. Maybe he had a stop to make before they left town.

But Jedidiah didn't stop, and unease churned in Sampson's gut as they left Missoula behind. When Jedidiah did something unexpected, it almost never boded well. He didn't dare ask the man where they were going. He'd seen more than one fellow beaten unconscious for questioning their boss—even if it were asked out of simple curiosity.

The wagon creaked under the weight of the supplies, each bump in the road jostling Sampson's already tense nerves.

Were they headed back to McPharland's mine? This road traveled that direction, but it also was the beginning of the route to his family's ranch. If only Jedidiah would give a hint of their destination.

The one thing he knew for certain was that they weren't

going toward the place where he'd parked the blasting powder the other night. Which meant Jedidiah had something else up his sleeve.

The sun dipped below the horizon. With trees on either side of the road blocking the dusky light, it felt like hours had passed. Jedidiah remained silent, his posture straight and his eyes fixed on the path ahead.

Maybe he should ask Jedidiah how far they planned to go tonight. He could pretend he was wondering about the horses.

Before he could voice the question, Jedidiah raised a hand for him to follow, then turned his mount onto a path.

Sampson's pulse picked up speed as he guided the wagon off the road, the wheels bouncing over rocks and roots. This was the general direction of his family's ranch, but at least a half hour before their usual turnoff from the main road. Surely that wasn't his destination.

Did Jedidiah even know where he was going? This didn't look like a trail at all. Would it be passable for the wagon? Turning the rig around might be impossible it they got in too far.

He had to make sure. He raised his voice so Jedidiah would hear. "Will there be room for the wagon ahead?"

The man didn't look back, but waved him forward and shouted something that might have been, "Yep."

The dense forest closed in around them, the shadows deepening with each passing moment. Branches scraped like clawing fingers against the wagon's sides.

At least a quarter hour passed, but then a glow appeared through the trees ahead. Was that the faint remaining sunlight in a clearing? Or a campfire?

As they drew closer, the glow turned into the flickering light of several fires. Through the trees, he could see men milling around.

Jedidiah didn't hesitate, just rode toward the group. He must know them. Probably, he'd brought them all here. But why so many? And why here? The knot in Sampson's belly twisted tighter.

Were these all miners Jedidiah had hired to help break ground on the new prospect? This was the wrong location though. They had to be at least three hours' ride from where the man had told Sampson to leave the blasting powder.

This was closer to the Coulter ranch, though still six or seven hours away, if he had his bearings right.

Surely this wasn't the beginnings of the dreaded attack on his family's mine that he'd been preparing for.

As the trees broke and he reached the little clearing where the men gathered, Sampson pulled back on the reins, bringing the wagon to a halt at the edge of a small clearing.

A quick scan of the group showed close to thirty men, some huddled around the campfires, others checking their weapons or tending horses. The air crackled with a tense energy, a sense of anticipation that set his nerves on edge.

The murmur of conversation died down as all eyes turned to the newcomers. A few faces looked familiar. Was that Albert? And Joe? The Wilcox brothers, a pair of bullies Jedidiah had used as henchman at Mick's mine. Those were the two who'd beaten Gil.

Most of the men he didn't know had the look of hardened drifters or outlaws. Not miners.

Jedidiah dismounted and strode into the midst of a small cluster, exchanging a few short greetings.

Sampson remained on the wagon bench. Maybe he should move in closer. Try to hear what Jedidiah said.

He set the brake and lowered himself to the ground. No one paid him much attention, and he was cold enough he'd be crazy not to want the warmth of one of the fires.

He strolled toward the blaze Jedidiah stood beside, keeping

himself on the outskirts of the men gathered around their leader.

"...brought the powder?" Jedidiah spoke in a low voice.

"Yep. Parked where you said." The man who answered had a deeper voice than average. Sampson glanced from the corner of his eye but couldn't tell if the one who'd spoken was the fellow wearing the coonskin cap or the one with the curly red beard.

The powder they spoke of...was that gunpowder? Or the same load Sampson had dropped off last night? Had that errand been a distraction to keep him guessing about the real plan?

Jedidiah spoke again, but his voice hummed lower, so Sampson missed some of the words. "...move out at first light....time to drop the powder...dark...strike...night."

A weight pressed so hard on Sampson's chest that he could barely breathe. *Strike.*

An attack.

And if they rode out at first light, they'd arrive at his family's ranch right before dark.

He had to act fast, to find a way to delay or derail their plans. But how? He was outnumbered and outgunned, with no way to warn his family.

And Grace and Ruby still waited for him in Missoula. If he didn't make it back...

No. He couldn't think like that. He had to focus on the task at hand, on finding a way to buy more time.

Maybe he could try the "mine played out" idea. If it worked, he'd be eternally grateful, for there'd be no doubt God played a hand in the miracle.

Sampson just had to get Jedidiah alone to tell him.

The man seemed to be mostly done talking business. After another minute, he looked around. "Where's the best stewpot?"

"That'd be Dawson's, one fire over." The red-bearded man said this in a voice no deeper than most. In fact, he spoke with a bit of a lilt, as if he came from Scotland or some such. Coonskin must have been the one reporting about the powder.

Jedidiah pushed through the crowd as he moved toward the campfire that had been pointed out. Once there, he picked up a tin bowl from the stack and ladled stew from the massive pot hanging on a tripod near the flames.

Sampson eased over to him, stopping beside Jedidiah like he was waiting his turn. He had to speak quickly, before the man walked off to find a seat.

Lord, help me. He grabbed his courage by the throat and charged in. "I was thinking…"

Jedidiah didn't show an obvious sign of listening, but he didn't move away, though he held a full bowl.

Sampson pressed on. "I'm not sure exactly what you have planned here, but I have a bit of information you might be interested in."

Jedidiah grunted. A sound that could mean a lot of things, but he would assume it meant for him to keep talking.

"My family's ranch is a little less than a day's ride from here, to the southeast. We've got a sapphire mine, but it's pretty much played out." He'd never actually talked to Mick or Jedidiah about the mine or the wagonload of sapphires they stole from his family, so it was probably best to pretend he knew nothing about it for this conversation. That way, Jedidiah couldn't pick up on bitterness in his tone.

The man glanced sideways at Sampson. "What's your point, boy?"

Sampson's heart pounded, but he kept his expression neutral. "There's another vein of sapphires, richer than the first, on some land just past our property line. I stumbled across it a few months back, but I haven't told anyone about it."

Jedidiah's eyes gleamed with interest, but suspicion lingered in his gaze. "And you're telling me this now because…?"

Sampson shrugged, trying to appear nonchalant. "I figure if you're planning something big, you might want to know about a better source to go after."

A slow, unsettling smile spread across Jedidiah's weathered face. He raised his free hand and clapped it on Sampson's shoulder, his grip uncomfortably tight.

"That's good to know, boy. Real good. I'll keep it in mind." His tone was genial, but there was a hard edge beneath the words that made Sampson's skin prickle with unease.

Jedidiah leaned in closer, his odor rank. "But we're after something much better than sapphires. And you've just made it clear where your loyalties lie."

Ice flooded Sampson's veins. He tried to step back, but Jedidiah's grip on his shoulder tightened, holding him in place.

"I can't have that kind of weakness in our midst." His voice came low and cold. The sound Sampson had heard too many times.

He should have known to brace for the blow.

A force slammed into the back of his knees, shoving him forward. Into the fire.

His thigh hit the tripod holding the stewpot. The entire contraption plunged into the flame, partially protecting him from the blaze. But heat scalded his hand when it pressed against the hot metal.

He struggled to roll sideways, out of the fire. A boot struck his head, sending an explosion of pain and light through his skull.

Someone grabbed his arm, jerking him up. He tried to find footing, but a fist plunged into his belly.

He couldn't catch his breath, couldn't pull up straight. Couldn't think or see. Another blow struck his face.

Jedidiah's hard voice hummed from a distance. "I can't abide a traitor. Teach him a lesson. Then get rid of him."

The hits rained harder. He curled in as much as they'd let him.

God, help me. Help my family. And protect Grace.

CHAPTER 9

*S*ampson gasped as a bolt of white-hot agony seared his middle, jerking him from sleep. He reached to grip his belly, but pain shot through his shoulder. What in the Rocky Mountains had happened to him?

Panic gripped his chest as he struggled to piece together fragmented memories. He worked to push his eyelids open. One wouldn't budge, but the other lifted to a hazy blur of dim light and flickering shadows. The light intensified the pounding in his head, and he let the eye close again.

Something soft rubbed against his hands. His cheeks too. But an icy chill nipped at his nose and brow. The air held the scent of a nearby fire.

Where was he? What had happened?

A voice cut through the fog clouding his mind. "Sampson? You are waking?" A familiar voice. Deep. With a lilt. It brought the feeling of happy adventures. Safe times.

Two Stones.

Squinting against the stabbing pain in his skull, he forced the eye open again and shifted his head.

Two Stones knelt beside him, his dark eyes filled with

concern. A hint of a smile touched his lips. "I am glad you have come back to us, my friend."

Sampson forced a swallow, his raw throat burning. His mouth felt like cotton, but he managed to get out a few words. "What happened?" His voice came out as a hoarse whisper.

Two Stones shook his head. "You made your friends very angry. It was not an easy task to get you away from them."

He strained for memory. He'd been…in Missoula Mills. Then driving the wagon. Jedidiah. They'd turned off the road… then…nothing.

"Heidi has gone for Dinah and Jericho." Two Stones reached for something, then moved a wooden bowl into his line of sight. "They will want to help bring you back to the ranch. But there has been a great snow. They may be slow in coming."

He spooned a liquid from the bowl and placed it at Sampson's lips. "Drink."

He obeyed, and a warm liquid dripped into his mouth. Swallowing burned, but some of the cotton cleared from his tongue.

As Two Stones refilled the spoon, Sampson focused on the man's words. The ranch. He couldn't leave…

With a jolt, memories rushed in. Grace. And Ruby. He started to push up, but his middle screamed in protest.

"Lie still, brother." Two Stones's voice left no room for argument. "You will make the wounds worse."

He couldn't get up anyway, so he sank back to the bed. A fur, now that he thought about it. They were outside, but Two Stones had built a small three-sided hut to shield him from the cold. And the snow.

He let himself lie there, eye closed, as he thought through what he could do. He'd been injured. Beaten, if he had to guess. He must have angered Jedidiah. How? That memory wouldn't come.

Thank the Lord Two Stones found him. How had that come about? He could ask in a minute.

First, he had to think through what would be best for Grace and the baby. If Jedidiah was angry with him, would he do something to Grace? It didn't seem likely a man would take something like that out on his own daughter, but he'd put nothing past Jedidiah.

He had to get them to a safe place, somewhere her father couldn't find them.

Another rented room in Missoula? He didn't know anyone there well enough to trust with such a critical task.

And if Jedidiah caught wind of where they were… Not only would Grace and Ruby not be safe, but whoever sheltered them would end up in the same condition Sampson was. Or worse.

He forced his eye open again to make sure Two Stones was close enough to hear. The man lifted another spoonful of liquid, but Sampson spoke before he could make him drink. "I need you to do something for me."

Two Stones's brow lifted, and he paused the spoon.

"Go to…Missoula. The hotel. Room one." His lungs could barely draw in a half breath, and he had to pause every few words. "My wife…and baby. Make sure…they're safe. Tell them…what happened. Bring them to…the ranch."

Two Stones didn't show the surprise he'd expected. But he'd always been good at concealing his reactions. His expression seemed humored more than anything, with the corners of his eyes creasing.

"I wondered what kept you away. I see now it is the way of all men."

Sampson would have grinned if it didn't hurt so much. He'd certainly not planned to come back with a wife and babe. He'd no doubt get some ribbing from his brothers.

Would Grace even agree to go back to the ranch? She'd made it clear she wanted to live by herself. This could be a temporary situation, until they could make sure she'd be safe from her father.

Still...Two Stones would have to convince her of that fact. Good thing Sampson had told her about this friend. Would she need proof that Sampson had indeed sent him? Proof that the danger was dire enough she should do as he was asking? Probably, but what could he send?

He opened his mouth for another spoonful of the drink as he thought through options. "My shirt...it was torn? And bloody?"

Two Stones glanced at Sampson's belly, though it felt like a fur covered him. "Yes."

Would Grace remember him leaving in that shirt? It might not be enough. Was there something else? Something in his belongings?

"Do you have my possibles sack?" He would have taken it with him in the wagon.

A frown flitted across Two Stones's face. "I took only your body when they thought you dead, or nearly so."

Sampson frowned, but the action made his entire face throb even more. "Who is *they*?"

"The men who beat you. Two big men. They went back to the fires after leaving you."

The two big men must have been Jedidiah's guards. Fires? He vaguely remembered the glow of several campfires. But straining so hard made the rest of his thoughts muddle.

He didn't have his sack. So what else could he send? A message? Maybe just telling Two Stones all the details about what had happened between him and Grace would be enough.

He took in as deep a breath as he could manage and started in. "You have to leave now to get Grace and the baby. If her father gets to her first, she might be in danger. Tell her...tell her what happened to me. Tell her I angered her father, and she and the baby are in danger. Tell her I know she didn't want to go to the ranch, but it's the only place safe right now. Make sure you bring the goat from the livery." He sucked in a breath, ignoring the fresh burn in his ribs. "Take her and the baby straight to the ranch. We'll meet you."

Two Stones studied him as he spoke, and even now when he'd finished. Why wasn't he moving?

Sampson did his best to glare. "Go now. You can't wait."

"Drink this first." He put a hand behind Sampson's head, and Sampson obediently lifted to drink from the bowl. He swallowed hard, pushing back the pain, until the full contents were gone.

As he lay back, his belly roiled. He was going to cast every bit of the drink back up. But maybe Two Stones would leave first.

His friend moved something beside Sampson. "Here is stew. More food in bag. Wood beside fire."

"Thank you." He finally let his body release the tension that had been fueling him.

Yet there was one thing more. "If she's not sure I sent you, tell her…" He struggled for what would be important to her. "I met her near McPharland's mine, where her father, Jedidiah, works. She was changing the babe's diaper. I offered her a ride in my wagon to her father in Missoula. She told me about Ruby, that someone left the babe for her to raise. That night, we had to stay in that old trapper's cabin near the Mullan Road." What more could he tell? Something very specific. "I heated ham and biscuits for us to eat that night." There, that should make her certain. Maybe he should add the last important detail, maybe more for Two Stones than Grace. "When we reached her father in Missoula, he made a show of us spending the night together and told us we had to marry. The deputy did our ceremony there in the hotel parlor."

Saying so much had wiped out the very last of his strength, but he didn't let himself close his eye yet. Instead, he watched Two Stones to see if the man had any questions.

He only nodded. "I will tell her."

After throwing more logs on the flames, Two Stones stared

at him one more time. "I will come back this way. If she comes willingly, we will see you before dark."

The thought of Grace seeing him this helpless pressed. And the snow and cold wouldn't be good for the babe. "Just get her safely to the ranch."

"God be with you, friend."

"And you." His voice broke with the words. *God, let Grace be safe. Help Two Stones get there in time.*

~

*G*race clutched Ruby close as she ducked through the hotel doors, out of the wind and snow still falling outside. She paused in the hallway to catch her breath and uncover the babe. They'd stopped at the livery on their way back from eating the midday meal at the café. Ruby loved to see the horses and goat, and Grace needed to keep busy while she waited for Sampson's return.

Where could he be? He'd been gone all night and morning, somewhere with her father. When he left, he'd said he expected to return before daylight.

The livery man said Sampson drove a full wagon, and her father rode horseback. With the heavy snowfall, maybe they'd gotten stuck somewhere.

Ruby fussed, her tiny face scrunching as it turned red. She needed a clean diaper and to eat, then likely a nap. Grace moved toward the stairs, but the hotel clerk called out, halting her.

"Mrs. Coulter?"

"Yes?"

He nodded toward the door on the opposite side of the hall. "You have a visitor, ma'am. He's waiting in the parlor."

Grace's heart leapt. Could it be Sampson? But why would he wait in the parlor instead of going up to their room? This parlor was where they'd been married. Did he have something special planned? Something to make up for being gone so much longer than he'd said?

A silly notion. She'd be disappointed if she started imagining things like that.

With her heart pounding, she crossed the lobby to the door that led to the sitting area. She pushed it open slowly, holding her breath as she peeked around the edge.

A tall figure stood near the fireplace. Not Sampson.

Not her father either. In fact, she didn't recognize this man at all.

He must have heard her, for he turned to face her. An Indian? Or, maybe part Indian.

His long dark hair was tied back, and he dressed in leathers like some of the other men around here.

She stayed in the doorway. Was it safe to be alone with him?

"Grace Coulter?" His voice hummed deep, and he spoke in clear English, though there might be a hint of an accent.

"Yes?" She clutched Ruby a little closer, which made the babe start fussing again.

"I am Two Stones. A friend of Sampson." He took a step closer, and those dark eyes homed on her. "He is hurt. Attacked by men who work for your father."

She sucked in a breath. No. "What do you mean? Where is he?" She leaned against the door frame, suddenly too weary to stand without help.

Hurt by her father? That couldn't be possible. There must have been an accident like she'd feared.

"I found him left for dead. He is awake and worried for you, his new wife." His gaze dropped to the bundle in her arms. "And daughter."

So many questions swirled inside her. Too many. She couldn't breathe well enough to think clearly. "Dead? How?"

The man's expression softened, and he stepped back as he

motioned to the sofa. "He is not dead. But hurt badly. Sit. I will tell all I know."

She needed to sit. Ruby had begun to nuzzle her neck, begging for food. She had nothing to feed her with. The babe would have to wait.

As she moved to the seat he'd indicated, she worked to pull her thoughts together. Sampson was hurt. And this man... She eyed him while she settled, turning the babe to face outward.

Sampson had talked of his family's native friend, the one who came when they first moved to the mountains. Two Stones had been the name. But maybe she should have this man confirm those details, just to make sure she could trust him.

She released a breath to level her voice. "How do you know my husband?"

The man also sat, facing her as he rested on the edge of an arm chair. "I have known him since the first days his family came to this land. His father was a father to me. He taught me of his God, and He is my God too. Sampson and his brothers are my brothers." He gripped his hands together in a firm clasp.

She eased out a breath. That's exactly what Sampson had said. Even the part about God.

The man kept talking. "In the night, I heard the sound of fighting. Of voices. I go closer and see two men beating another. They see he is no more and leave him. I knew the man on the ground. My brother, Sampson." He pressed a hand to his chest. "He is alive, and my wife gave him the shelter I made for her. She has gone to get his family. When Sampson wakes, he does not remember all. But he begged me to come to you. To bring you and the babe to his family. He will meet you there. You will be safe with the Coulters."

She had to strain to follow his story, between the slight accent and the unusual way he worded things. She could barely sort through her own thoughts too. He had to be speaking the truth. He knew too much about their situation.

Which meant Sampson must really be hurt. Emotion rose in her throat. "Is it bad? Are there injuries?" She yearned for him to say no. That Sampson had awakened with only a few bruises.

Two Stones dipped his chin. "I could not tell which bones are broken. But he is in much pain. His sister Dinah is a doctor. She will come to help."

Grace had to go to him. Had to do everything she could for him. She started to push to her feet, but Ruby in her arms made her pause. She couldn't take Ruby out there, could she? Yet there was no one here to leave her with.

Two Stones leaned forward. "I am to bring you and your daughter to the Coulter ranch. Jericho and Dinah will bring Sampson there to meet you."

She studied him. That might be better. *If* she could trust this man to take her there.

He definitely seemed to be Sampson's friend. But the thought of leaving town, of riding out into the wilderness with a stranger...it terrified her.

She met Two Stones's gaze, searching for any hint of deception. "How do I know you're telling me the truth? That Sampson really sent you?"

The man's expression remained calm and earnest. "He said you might doubt me. That is why he told me things only he would know. Like how you met him near the mine where your father worked. You were changing the child's soiled clothes. You stayed that night in the old cabin near the road. Sampson heated ham and biscuits to eat that night. Then when you came to your father, he forced the marriage between you." His eyes drifted to Ruby. "Sampson said the child is not yours by blood, but that you love her as your own."

Assurance spread through her with every new fact. There was no way someone would know all those things unless Sampson had told him.

She nodded, then stood, adjusting Ruby in her arms. "I need to feed her and pack our things."

Two Stones nodded, rising as well. "I will ready the horses and goat and bring them here."

Sampson had even thought to mention the goat.

But horses. She'd never been a confident rider, and with Ruby... "I don't know if I can manage on horseback with a baby. Is there not a wagon we can use?"

"A wagon will not make it through the snow. The trails are treacherous now." Two Stones must have seen the fear on her face, for his tone softened. "Do not worry. I will help with the child. And the mare I secured for you has a gentle temper."

Grace gave a reluctant nod. "All right. I'll be as quick as I can."

CHAPTER 10

*S*ampson huddled beneath the furs, his breath forming clouds in the frigid air. Pain throbbed through every limb. He gritted his teeth against it. At least the snow had stopped falling. The crackling fire sent a fair amount of heat to this makeshift shelter where Two Stones had left him.

Worry gnawed at his belly, almost as intense as the pain in his ribs and left shoulder. Were Grace and little Ruby all right? Had Jedidiah returned to Missoula to have his lackeys do something awful to them?

He had to stop worrying or he'd drive himself mad. Two Stones would get them out. Surely. God had brought the man in time to save Sampson's life, so surely He'd be there for Grace and Ruby as well.

Besides, Sampson had other concerns to focus on. This late in the afternoon, Jericho and Dinah might arrive soon, if they'd pushed hard.

He wasn't altogether certain they'd do that, though. His family might have given up on him by now. Decided he wasn't worth so much extra effort. He'd been gone for months, and the few times he'd seen one of them, he'd taken pains to tell them to steer clear of him. To leave him alone and go home.

Really, he'd just needed them to stay as far away from McPharland and Jedidiah as possible. The entire operation was dirty. He'd planned to find their weaknesses himself and stop them, but he couldn't let anyone he loved get hurt. Gil had already paid the price. Thank the Lord he'd gotten away with only a beating.

McPharland had been furious at Gil's escape, especially when his brother took the man's daughter with him. He didn't forgive and forget well. Sampson'd had to prove his loyalty to Jedidiah even more after that fiasco.

The crunch of hooves in the snow jolted him from the turmoil of those memories. He reached for the rifle on the fur beside him. He'd already propped himself up enough to see anyone who approached…and shoot if he needed to.

A voice drifted through the trees—a woman's. He eased out a breath. Then Jericho's strong baritone sounded, and Sampson's chest tightened again. He laid the gun aside.

He would have to face them.

The riders appeared through the trees—Jericho, Dinah, and Heidi. She must be exhausted after riding all the way to the ranch and back, probably without a rest.

Jericho stepped into the circle of the camp first, then halted as he took in Sampson, lying in the shelter. Dinah pressed through just behind her husband, but she didn't stop to study him. Just charged forward with a bag slung over her shoulder.

The widening of her eyes as she drew near told him just how bad he must look. "Sampson. What's happened to you?" She dropped to her knees by his side.

He managed a weak smile. "Good to see you, too, Dinah." The words rasped out, his throat raw from the cold.

She frowned, her face etched with concern as she reached for the furs covering him. "Let me see."

He flinched, more from the gentleness in her voice than any pain. "It's not as bad as it looks."

She ignored his words, just pulled back the fur to see his upper body. "Where does it hurt? Heidi said something about your arm and ribs?"

Two Stones must have seen swelling in those areas. The man knew his way around an injury.

"Just my ribs and that left shoulder." He glanced down at the spot but couldn't see much with that left eye swollen nearly shut.

Jericho stepped closer, his expression tight. "Where's Two Stones?"

Sampson shifted as Dinah pressed on his shoulder. He had to fight to keep from jerking away from the pain. From crying out. Through a clenched jaw, he managed to speak. "I sent him to Missoula. Someone's there who...might not be safe...without me around."

He had to focus on breathing to keep the pain from blinding him. Dinah had stopped touching the arm, but his ribs pounded with a fury now.

Dinah was probing them, but thankfully, she kept her touch lighter this time.

Jericho's spoke again, but Sampson squeezed his eyes shut as he focused on each breath in and out. "Should I go after him to help?"

Sampson shook his head, though that might have been a poor choice, considering how it made his head throb. "No." He managed to push the word out, and finally Dinah moved her poking down to his belly. There couldn't be broken bones down there. Just bruises, from the feel of it.

Jericho held his tongue, but that didn't mean the questioning was over. At least Sampson didn't have to face both tortures at the same time.

After Dinah worked her way down his legs, she sat back on

81

her heels. "These ribs are definitely broken. And your shoulder...it looks like there's a break." Her gaze shifted to his face. "We'll wrap your abdomen and brace the arm against your body. After that, do you feel up to riding back to the ranch?"

No. Not for a few months at least. "Sure." He didn't have a choice, did he?

"It'll be dark soon." Jericho stepped in once more. "Might be best to get a good night sleep and start back in the morning."

"I'll give you something for the pain, then we can clean and bandage you." Dinah turned to open the satchel at her side.

Pain medicine. That was the best news he'd had all day.

After Dinah had him swallow a liquid, Heidi brought a pot from the fire to place beside him. "This water should cool quickly." When she glanced up at Sampson's face, she winced.

He must really look rough.

Jericho crouched by his head, and Sampson tipped his chin up to see his eldest brother. With his swollen eyes, he couldn't focus enough to gauge Jericho's gaze—a small blessing.

"Who did this to you, little brother?" For once, Jericho's voice wasn't hard and commanding. It held a tenderness Sampson hadn't heard in years.

"I...don't know. I can't remember." That was a truth he could be thankful for just now.

"Do you have an idea? An inkling?" Jericho sounded patient, but he didn't seem to buy the amnesia excuse.

Dinah lifted his shirt and began rubbing a wet cloth over his belly. Sampson sucked in a breath. Though the water was warm, the moment the icy air hit his damp skin, it felt like it turned into icicles.

"Sorry," she murmured. "I'll be quick." She was rubbing at a particularly sore spot, and he had to grit his teeth to keep from pushing her away.

At least his shoulder didn't hurt quite as bad. Maybe the medicine was working already.

"What's the last thing you recall?" Jericho wouldn't give up with the questions.

He let his eyes close again. "I was driving a wagon. Out of Missoula." He strained for more. He could decide whether he'd tell his brother anything else if he remembered new details, but...nothing came.

He opened his eyes. "I can't remember anything after that."

Jericho squinted at him, definitely not liking the answer. "Do you have a sense whether the man who beat you was a stranger on the road or someone you knew?" He still didn't sound angry. Maybe more worried than anything.

"I...don't know." That wasn't quite the truth. He was pretty sure Jedidiah had something to do with this. And he'd not mentioned the fact that Jedidiah was riding with him.

Jericho blew out a breath. His voice gentled when he spoke to his wife. "Anything I can do to help?"

She shook her head, lowering Sampson's shirt before she pulled the fur up over his belly. "I need to clean his face before we wrap him. It'll be a few minutes."

Sampson let his eyes drift shut. Sounded like he had plenty of fun coming. At least a bit of warmth had crept into his bones. And the hurt had begun to fade everywhere. Maybe once Dinah finished all her fussing, he could sleep.

Two Stones would be with Grace by now, and maybe they'd already left Missoula. She and Ruby were safe. Two Stones wouldn't let anyone touch them.

He could finally manage a full breath, and he drew in another dose of clear air. He'd have to tell his family about his marriage. Maybe Two Stones would do that for him if he reached the ranch first.

Sampson should tell Jericho and Dinah before then.

Tomorrow morning. He didn't have to give them all the details. They wouldn't understand, but they couldn't change anything.

And he didn't regret for a second making Grace his wife. The farther he could get her from her father, the safer she and the baby would be.

CHAPTER 11

*A*ccording to Two Stones, they were almost to the ranch. Traveling hadn't been as bad as Grace expected. Not that it'd been easy, but the journey without Two Stones would have been much harder. He'd anticipated almost everything she would need, each step of the way.

He'd made a sling to carry Ruby on his chest most of the time they rode, and the baby seemed content with that arrangement. When she grew hungry, he always stopped so Grace could feed and change her. They'd even spent the night in the same cabin she and Sampson had stayed in. Though she hadn't felt nearly as safe with the Indian, knowing Sampson had sent him helped her to relax in his presence.

As the trail maneuvered beside a rocky outcropping, she peered ahead to where it looked like the trees thinned. Two Stones said they would reach the main house soon. Maybe this was it. And was that the scent of wood smoke?

The trail opened into a wide clearing set on a hillside. A cabin sat in the middle with a barn down the slope. Smoke curled from the chimney of each building.

At the sight, Two Stones let out a low whistle.

Almost at the same instant, the cabin door opened and two men stepped out. Another emerged from the barn. They were all too far away for her to see what they looked like, but all held rifles.

Two Stones raised a hand, and that seemed to be a signal. The pair at the house started toward them, rifles lowering to their sides. So did the man from the barn. Then more from the house and another from around the back of the barn. Some of the people streaming from the buildings were women.

As the first few met them, her eyes couldn't find the right place to land. All the men bore a resemblance to Sampson—most of them anyway. That dark hair and those piercing brown eyes. The broad shoulders.

One of the men in front looked to Two Stones, his expression guarded. "Good to see you, friend. We've been worried. You brought company." His gaze slid to Grace. "Jericho and Dinah not with you?"

Two Stones shook his head. "Sampson asked me to go on to Missoula to bring his wife and babe ahead to the ranch." He turned to Grace, as though he'd not just poured kerosine into a fire. "This is Grace." He motioned to the child strapped to his chest. "And Ruby."

She forced herself to look up to see their reactions. Surprise for sure. But not anger. Not at first glimpse anyway.

The man who'd first spoken turned to her. "Welcome to the Coulter ranch, Grace. You're a surprise, but not an unwelcome one." He took a step back and motioned them forward. "Come to the house and let's get you settled."

That was it? Surely not the only explanation she'd need to give, but the family's first reaction was so much kinder than she'd expected. Of course, they were Sampson's kin. Maybe she should have expected them to be like him.

She hated to imagine her father's reaction to such a surprise.

Her horse followed behind Two Stones's as it had all the

hours on the trail. When they stopped at the house, people gathered around, including a man at the mare's head and two women at Grace's side. Another fellow reached up to help her down.

The kindness in his eyes reminded her of Sampson. She allowed him to assist her as she dismounted, her legs stiff from the long ride.

Two Stones dismounted, too, and carefully unwrapped Ruby from the sling. Grace stepped close to take the babe. She needed the familiar warmth of this child in her arms.

"She's adorable."

Grace glanced over to see a young woman around her own age peering at Ruby's sleepy expression. The woman's gaze shifted to meet Grace's, and a shyness settled in her eyes. "I'm Jess. I have my own little one coming soon." She glanced down at the swell she cradled with one hand.

"Congratulations." Grace managed a smile. A baby was wonderful news, but Grace was so weary. And all these people… She needed a quiet place to gather herself.

And change Ruby's clothing. Keeping her clean had been hard on the trail. She needed a wet cloth and a new gown posthaste.

"Let's get you inside where it's warm." Another woman spoke, touching Grace's shoulder.

She allowed herself to be guided up a couple of steps toward the door, her legs unsteady after so many hours in the saddle.

Grace stepped in to the warm and inviting cabin, holding Ruby close to her chest. A fire crackled in the hearth to the left, and chairs were grouped in a homey scene before it. On the far right sat a cookstove and a massive dining table. The scent of something savory made her stomach rumble.

The whole place had been decorated with garland and bows.

Realization slammed into her. Was today Christmas? Or yesterday? She'd lost track of the days with so much happening.

"You must be hungry and cold." A kind-faced woman with red hair stood before her. "Do you want to sit by the fire, and I'll bring you a bowl of soup?"

She couldn't worry about the holiday right now. She glanced at Ruby, then back to the woman. "I... Is there a place I can change her? And maybe some warm water?"

"Of course." Another woman stepped into view, this one with dark blonde hair. "Come back to one of the bed chambers and we'll get her settled."

Grace followed her to one of the two doors on the far wall. They stepped into the room on the right, the woman motioning to the big double bed. "That should be a good place to lay her. This is my sister and Jericho's room, but they've both gone to help Sampson. You can have the place to yourself. I'm Naomi, by the way. I'll bring warm water. Would you like a big pot to bathe her in? Sometimes it helps to dunk instead of trying to wipe all those rolls and creases."

A bit of weight eased from Grace's shoulders, and she offered a smile that came much easier. "That would be wonderful."

Naomi smiled, her eyes crinkling at the corners. "Do you need clothes for her? Clean diapers? I remember how quickly a babe goes through those things. And it's nearly impossible to do laundry on the trail."

This woman must have a child or two of her own. She certainly possessed the comforting, gentle manner of a mother. How long before Grace developed that trait? Did you have to actually give birth to a child to have that mother's demeanor?

She pushed the worries away and shook her head. "I have what I need in my pack." Which was still strapped on the saddle. She wrinkled her nose. "Would someone be able to bring it in? Or...I can go get it."

Naomi turned to the door. "The men already brought that. I'll be right back."

She left the door open, but it wasn't hard to block out the activity in the other room. Grace glanced around this chamber. The oldest brother's room. The master and mistress of the house. It felt like she shouldn't be in here. She certainly shouldn't touch anything.

She had to get Ruby cleaned up though. She'd do it quickly, then move out by the fire to feed the babe. For now, she'd best not lay her on the bed until she could remove this damp gown.

A moment later, the red-haired woman stepped in with a stack of cloths and Grace's satchel. "The water is heating, both for you and the babe. We thought a bath might be a good way to get you warm too. Miles and Eric are bringing the tub in now."

A bath. Oh, how she longed to be clean and warm again. The idea of soaking in hot water seemed almost too good to be true after so many days.

"Thank you," she managed, emotion thickening her voice. "That's very kind."

The woman's smile deepened, her eyes filled with under-standing. "I'm Patsy, Jonah's intended. We're so glad to have you here, Grace. Sampson is…well, he's special to all of us. Anyone important to him is important to us too."

Tears pricked at Grace's eyes, and she blinked to hold them back. The easy acceptance, the warm welcome—they touched a place deep inside her, soothing hurts she hadn't even realized she carried.

Naomi stepped in behind Patsy. "We're actually going to move you to the room over, if you don't mind sharing it with Clara. The men are taking the tub and water in there."

She moved farther into the room, and her eyes warmed even more. "Would you trust me to bathe your sweet one? I have a daughter of my own who was once this tiny, though it's hard to believe it now. She's two years old and so big."

Grace swallowed the worry that niggled in her chest. If

Naomi had birthed her own child, surely she would be far more capable than Grace.

Naomi seemed to understand her hesitation. "We'll be right there near you in case Ruby needs her mama. I'd like to give you a chance to tend to yourself, though." The crinkles at the corners of her eyes deepened. "And honestly, I'm longing to hold that sweet wee one. My Mary Ellen has grown so."

Grace eased out a breath as she nodded. "Thank you."

Within a few minutes, they'd moved to the next chamber over that contained two single beds. A large tub filled the empty space at the far end, and several men carried buckets of water in every few minutes. Grace had handed Ruby off to Naomi, and Jess and another dark-haired woman named Angela were assisting her as they unwrapped the babe from her dirty trappings.

"There's a sweet girl." Naomi cooed as she hovered above the bed. She held Ruby's head in one hand, the babe's body along her arm, as she unwound the wet diaper from around those tiny hips. The move looked so familiar, so practiced, and a bit of tension eased out of Grace. She'd already pulled Ruby's things out of their satchel and laid them on the bed beside Naomi. They should have everything they needed.

Including plenty of helping hands. Angela looked to be in the family way, as Jess was, so both of them surely had the same mothering instincts as Naomi.

One of the men entered the room with a large steaming pot, and Patsy followed him. He poured the contents into the tub, then stepped back. "I think that'll do it."

Before she could offer a "thank you," he left the room, closing the door behind him. Patsy tugged a folding partition from against the wall and placed it between the bed and wash-tub. "There." She turned back to smile at Grace. "Anything else I can bring you? There's soap and a towel there." She nodded to the items on a bureau nearby. "Do you need a clean gown?

Anything?" She motioned toward the other women. "Between us, I'm sure we could find one to fit."

Grace managed a smile, swallowing a lump of emotion. "This is more than enough. Thank you." She wanted desperately to tuck herself behind that screen and sink into the warm water. Alone.

Was it wrong that she craved a break from her daughter, from all the voices and chaos?

Probably.

Patsy's knowing gaze told Grace she understood. Her smile communicated a complete lack of judgment. "Take your time. We'll have a warm meal ready for you when you're finished."

Though the women hadn't left, Grace slipped behind the partition and shed her dirty clothes, leaving them in a heap on the floor. Then she stepped into the tub, sinking down into the deliciously hot water with a sigh.

Bliss. Utter, pure bliss. The heat seeped into her weary muscles, unknotting the tension and washing away the aches. She laid back, resting her head against the curved edge, and closed her eyes.

For long minutes, she simply soaked, letting her mind drift.

Distantly, she heard the women's soft chatter as they tended to Ruby, but the words were muffled, indistinct. All that registered was the gentle timbre of their voices, the occasional gurgle from the babe. Sounds of comfort and attention.

What would it be like to live in a place like this, surrounded by the love and care she'd been immersed in since reaching this house? A life where Ruby would grow up knowing the affection of family?

A rush of moisture stung her eyes, and she squeezed them shut. She couldn't let herself get used to this. She'd told Sampson she wanted independence.

And anyway, right now, these kind people thought Sampson had married her because he loved her. When she told them that her father had forced him into it, they'd not be so keen on accepting her and Ruby into their midst.

She let out a quiet sigh. She had to tell them soon. Right after she climbed out of this glorious bath and made herself decent.

With that thought firmly planted in her mind, she braced for disappointment and reached for the bar of soap.

CHAPTER 12

*D*arkness pressed in on all sides as Sampson clung to his saddle, his eyelids heavy as lead. Each jarring step of the horse sent a fresh wave of pain rippling through his battered body. Only Dinah's laudanum kept him upright, but it came at the price of exhaustion thick as molasses.

Home. His bed in the bunkhouse. Just a little farther…

Jericho had ridden ahead to alert the others, and as they entered the yard, lantern light glimmered from up by the house. It must be close to bedtime, but a group of people had gathered.

His family.

The knot in his middle tightened. He wasn't ready to face them. Not yet. Not as miserable as he felt.

Heidi and Dinah rode toward the house, but he turned his gelding toward the barn and bunkhouse. He had no strength left to explain, to talk. He needed sleep first.

"Sampson, come up to the house," Dinah called, her voice laced with concern. "I'll make a bed for you there so I can be close if you need anything."

He fought to form words, to push them past his locked jaw. "Going…to bed. Talk…in the morning."

Dinah turned to ride with him. " I'd feel much better having you in the house. You can rest there."

Sampson shook his head, then hissed as pain lanced through his skull, the battered flesh of his face screaming in protest. He knew how rough he must look, how pitiful. And he couldn't bear to be fussed over, to be seen so weak.

He couldn't let the rest of his family see him like this. Especially if Grace and the baby were already here. "I'll be fine," he managed. "Have one of the boys bring the laudanum. I'll take it myself if I wake up hurting." They could tell him for sure that Grace and Ruby had arrived. He tried to push more strength into his voice. "I'll see everyone in the morning."

Dinah fell silent, and the sound of her mount's steps no longer trailed him. He kept riding, each step of the horse sending a fresh jolt of agony through his body. But also, the promise of relief. Almost there. Almost to the haven of sleep, where he could forget the pain, forget the mistakes that weighed like millstones around his neck.

For a few blissful hours, he could just rest. And maybe, if God was kind, he'd wake with the strength to face the consequences of his choices, to start setting things right. One woozy step at a time.

The barn loomed ahead, a hulking silhouette against the dark sky. He reined in his gelding, then gritted his teeth for the dismount. This was the worst part, since he couldn't use the bad arm and his ribs screamed when he tightened his middle. Gripping the saddle, he swung his leg over the horse and slid to the ground.

As his boots hit the dirt, pain exploded behind his eyes, and darkness swirled at the edges of his vision. He locked his knees, fighting the urge to crumple. Passing out face-first in horse manure would be a fitting end to this wretched day, but he'd not let it happen if he could help it.

"Sampson! Thank the Lord you're home." Miles appeared at his elbow, his face a mask of worry in the lantern light. "Let me help you inside."

Sampson forced a smile, hoping it looked less like a grimace. "Good to see you, little brother." The words scraped his raw throat. "Did Two Stones come with…?"

Talking used up so much energy, but hopefully Miles knew who he meant.

"With your wife and daughter? Yeah. Look forward to hearing that story." Miles's needling came through in his tone, but Sampson had no energy for it. Not now.

"They're fine?"

"Seem to be. Sleeping now I think. You want me to wake Grace?"

Sampson eyed the bunkhouse. "Nah. Mind putting my horse away? I need…"

A wave of dizziness crashed over him, and he swayed, grabbing the saddle for support.

Miles's hands shot out to steady him.

Sampson blinked hard, trying to clear his vision. He focused on putting one foot in front of the other as Miles guided him toward the bunkhouse. "I just…need to lie down."

He let his brother walk with him to the door, but when he tugged the latch open, he clung to the wood. "I've got it from here." He couldn't focus with his blurry vision to look Miles in the eye. "It's good to see you. We'll talk in the morning."

Miles didn't step back right away, but Sampson had no strength to wait for him to leave. He pushed the door shut, then stumbled toward the bunk that had always been his.

He had to rest. And if he was lucky enough to find sleep, he could shut out the world and its troubles. He could forget, just for a little while, the wrongs he needed to right. The laudanum tugged like a stubborn mule at his senses.

95

Bed. Oblivion.

Everything else could wait for dawn.

~

A feeble cry pierced Grace's sleep, and she forced her eyes open. Ruby needed to eat.

She squinted at the light coming through the window. Morning, which meant this wouldn't be a simple feeding then back to sleep. The babe would want to stay up and play.

She held in a sigh and pushed up to sitting, swinging her legs over the side of the bed.

Ruby's hungry fussing was turning more desperate, which meant she'd be wailing soon if Grace didn't hurry.

She moved to the basket and reached down for her. "It's all right, sweet one. We'll get you clean and fed. Don't cry." She scooped up the swaddled babe, cradling her close as Ruby's cries turned to shuddering breaths. "Shhh. I'm here."

A soft knock at the door made her pause. "Yes?" Had Ruby woken someone?

That brought another thought. *Clara.*

Grace spun to see if the woman whose room they were sharing was still asleep. She'd completely forgotten about Clara in the other bed.

But that cot lay empty, with the blankets pulled up neatly. Had Grace overslept? She eyed the light streaming through the window. It was later than she'd realized, but her body screamed that it couldn't possibly be time to stay awake for the day.

A soft voice sounded through the door. "It's me. Jess. I heard Ruby and wondered if I could help."

"Come in."

Ruby was starting to fuss again, bumping her mouth against Grace's neck in a desperate search for food.

Grace stepped to her bed and laid her down so she could

change her wet wrappings. "Let's get you clean. Then you can eat."

The door opened, and Jess peeked in.

Grace managed to lift a tight smile for her. "Good morning. I'm sorry if the noise bothered everyone."

Jess padded in with silent steps, her presence as gentle as her voice. "Not at all. I thought you might want a few minutes for yourself, so I hoped you'd let me change and feed Ruby."

Grace lifted her gaze to see if Jess was earnest in the offer. Take over everything the babe needed right now? That felt like an offer much bigger than Jess probably realized.

The other woman was already reaching for a clean diaper from the stack beside the basket. A stack one of the other women had washed, dried, folded, and brought back to the room.

It all felt like too much. Too wonderful.

She couldn't let herself get used to all this help, but maybe she could allow it just this morning.

She moved back to allow Jess room to work. "Thank you."

The other woman greeted Ruby with a smile as she set in to the task. "There's our sweet baby. Good morning. You're just so precious."

Jess would make a wonderful mother, with her soft manner and gentle ways. She was already pulling the hint of a smile from the babe, even with Ruby's hunger.

Grace took another step back. She had a few precious minutes to make herself presentable for the day ahead. She'd best use her time well.

As Grace unfastened her braid, Jess spoke up. "I heard Sampson came in near midnight with Dinah and Jericho."

Sampson.

A flutter slipped through her, but then worry took its place, clenching her gut. How badly was he injured? And if he was here, where was he staying? Was there a room here they used for a clinic? "Is he...how is he?"

Jess tugged the clean diaper into place. "I didn't see him myself. He's out in the bunkhouse. But Dinah said he's in rough shape. A broken arm near his shoulder. Several broken ribs. Lots of bruises and cuts."

Grace swallowed hard. She needed to see him. Needed to know exactly how dire his condition was. "May I go to him?"

Jess nodded as she swaddled Ruby again and picked her up. "I'm sure that would be fine. He might still be sleeping, but we could check with Dinah first."

Dinah. The woman everyone here spoke so highly of. A doctor and the wife of Sampson's eldest brother. What would she think of Grace coming into her home without permission?

By the time Jess had Ruby content and suckling the bottle, Grace had slipped into a dress, washed her face, and tidied her hair.

Jess smiled as she held the drinking babe, Ruby's bottom resting on the swell of Jess's own child. "Shall we go talk to Dinah?"

She took a deep breath and nodded. "I'm ready."

She followed Jess into the main room, scanning the space quickly to see who was here. She'd only heard the low murmur of voices.

A few women worked in the kitchen area. Patsy and Clara and...

A woman with striking blonde hair stood at the cookstove. She came toward them, a warm smile on her face. Grace's stomach twisted.

"You must be Grace." Dinah's voice was rich and kind. "We're so glad to have you here." She enfolded Grace in a warm, tight hug that wrapped all the way around her. So much like Mama's had been.

Tears surged, pushing hard. She sucked in a breath to hold

the grief back. She couldn't think of Mama or she'd lose her composure fully.

Her vision blurred, and she tried to focus on the fact that this was Sampson's sister-in-law. An important member of his family. Someone she needed to make a good impression on.

Dinah pulled back, but she surely saw Grace's tears. She kept hold of Grace's hands, her blue eyes full of compassion. "You've been through so much in such a short time, haven't you?"

How much had Sampson told them? Dinah's words held a question, and an invitation to share. Maybe she wondered what part of her recent experience had brought on the tears. Hopefully she didn't think marrying Sampson had contributed. She should tell this woman that the hug reminded her of her own mother. But speaking of Mama would send her into sobs, and she couldn't do that. Not right now.

She sniffed and worked for a smile to push back the emotion. "I'm sorry for coming into your home when you weren't here."

Dinah gave her hands a squeeze. "Please, don't apologize. You're family now. This is your home too."

The kindness and sincerity in the woman's clear blue eyes only made the tears threaten harder. Grace nodded, not trusting her voice.

Dinah seemed to sense her struggle and released her hands. "Sampson was quite stubborn about it, but he insisted on staying in the bunkhouse last night instead of in the house."

Fresh worry knotted in her middle. "How is he? Truly?"

"He looks worse than he is." Compassion lingered in her eyes, though her tone shifted to something more like a doctor would use to give a diagnosis. "None of his injuries should be life-threatening, praise God. He's in a great deal of pain. I'm giving him laudanum to help manage it for now, but he can't stay on that for long."

A heaviness seemed to hang on those last words, and Dinah's expression shadowed.

What would the laudanum do if Sampson took it too long? Was it dangerous even now?

She swallowed hard. "May I...go see him?"

"Of course. I'll take you." Dinah smiled. "I'm sure he'll love to see you." She turned toward the door. "Make sure you bundle up. It's a brisk walk to the bunkhouse."

CHAPTER 13

*G*race hesitated. Should she leave the baby?

Jess sat in a rocking chair near the hearth, feeding Ruby. She smiled up at Grace. "Go on. I'll take good care of this sweet angel."

It felt wrong to leave her child for someone else to care for. But Jess looked incredibly content, Ruby snuggled in the crook of her arm. A contentment Grace knew well. If she truly didn't mind caring for Ruby a little longer, it would be best not to take the babe out into the cold.

She murmured "thank you" and followed Dinah to the door, where she pulled her coat from a peg.

Once bundled, she followed Dinah into the brisk morning air. The sun shone bright and clear, but the wind held a biting chill that stung her cheeks as they made their way down the gentle slope toward the barn and bunkhouse.

Dinah glanced her way, her expression gentle like before. "It's not easy, is it? Letting others help care for your little one. Especially when you've had to shoulder it all alone."

The words pierced deep, and Grace's throat tightened. She could only manage a nod.

Dinah's eyes held a sheen of empathy. "You're not alone anymore, Grace. We're all here for you now. And for Ruby."

More tears burned, and she blinked hard. What had she done to deserve such kindness? Such a generous welcome from near strangers?

Before she could form a response, they reached the bunkhouse door.

Dinah gave a light knock as she pushed it open and poked her head in, then spoke in a hushed voice. "Good morning. I've brought Grace to see Sampson."

A male voice answered, his tone deep but quiet. "Come on in."

Dinah held the door wider and motioned Grace to go ahead.

She stepped into the dim interior, blinking as her eyes adjusted from the brightness outside.

A tall man stood between the two closest bunks, his dark hair and sharp eyes marking him as one of the Coulter men. Beside him was Sean, Sampson's eight-year-old nephew, whom she'd met yesterday.

She gave Sean a smile before focusing on the man.

The strong lines of his face softened. "You must be Grace. I'm Jericho, Sampson's brother. We're glad to have you here."

Another warm welcome. She'd not expected it from any of them, especially not this daunting man.

She worked for a smile. "Thank you. I'm sorry to impose on your family like this."

He waved off her words. "Family is never an imposition. You're a Coulter now, and we take care of our own." His gaze shifted to the lower bunk beside him, and his expression sobered. "Speaking of which, you've got your work cut out for you taking on this fellow as a husband."

Grace followed his gaze, and her heart lurched as she made out a form under the blankets. Only a tuft of Sampson's brown hair showed beyond the covers.

Dinah stepped closer and pulled back the blanket, speaking softly to rouse him. "Sampson? Your wife is here to see you."

Grace could hardly breathe, her stomach roiling as she took in the damage to his handsome face. The strong planes and angles she'd admired just two days before were now distorted, mottled black. His eyes had swollen to mere slits. If his family hadn't told her this was Sampson, she might not have recognized him.

Dinah motioned for Grace to come closer as she stepped back. "We'll give you some privacy. I'll be back in a little while to change his bandages."

After the couple and the boy left and the door closed with a soft click, silence filled the small building, broken only by Sampson's labored breathing.

She swallowed hard and took a small step toward the low bed, fighting the urge to run back out the door. Should she try to talk to Sampson? Or let him rest? What would help him most?

Before she could decide, one of his swollen eyelids parted just a slit, enough for him to peer at her. His puffy, split lips opened, but the voice that rasped out sounded nothing like his usual strong tone. "I'm sorry...you have to see me...like this." The words came slowly, and he stopped to breathe after every few.

She twisted her hands together. "I'm so sorry you're hurt. What happened?" Two Stones said her father had been involved. But surely he could never have done anything this brutal. Not to any man, and especially not to her husband.

His one half-open eye studied her a moment, filled with pain and some other heavy emotion she couldn't decipher. "Are you all right? And Ruby?"

Of course his first thought would be for her and the babe. Even in this terrible state. "We're fine. Two Stones brought us here safely."

Sampson's expression seemed to ease, though how she could determine that with so much swelling she had no idea. "He's a good friend. Did anyone...bother you...before he came?"

She shook her head. "No one."

"Good." His eye drifted closed, as if the conversation had drained him.

But he couldn't sleep yet. She had to know what caused this. Who was responsible for this horrible act. "Sampson, how did this happen?"

That one eyelid parted again. "Last thing I remember...is driving the wagon behind...your father's horse. He took us off... the main road."

Grace's heart clenched. "You don't remember who did this to you? Could my father be hurt too?" She should have thought of that possibility sooner.

Sampson's eye opened a little wider as he looked at her. Studying her or trying to remember? Was he wondering how much she could bear to hear?

She homed her gaze on him. "Please, tell me the truth. I need to know."

Sampson drew in a slow breath, his eye closing a moment before he opened it again to meet her look. "It's all...hazy. But I'm pretty sure...I must have done something...to anger him."

Him?

Him...as in her father?

Sampson paused, seeming to gather his strength to continue. "The condition I'm in...it's what happens...to someone who makes...Jedidiah angry. Even if unintentional."

Grace's chest turned to ice.

Her father had done this? Beaten Sampson—her husband—nearly to death? Because of some minor slight?

Sampson's gaze held hers, heavy with truth and pain. "It must not have been...too bad. I'm still alive."

Nausea roiled through her, and she pressed a hand to her

middle. Her father was capable of this level of violence? Of hurting her husband this severely?

She shook her head, fighting the thought. "No. He couldn't… My father would never…" But even as the denial left her lips, doubt sank deep hooks into her heart.

Sampson closed his eye. "I'm sorry, Grace. I don't remember…all the details. But I've seen…what your father does…to people who cross him. And the result looks…a lot like this." The air seemed to seep out of him, as if the revelation had drained him completely.

A sob caught in her throat, and she pressed a hand to her mouth as she sank down on the bunk across from Sampson's.

Had she missed his true nature all these years? He'd never been warm and doting like Mama. But she remembered how he used to smile when she was younger. When had he stopped smiling? She'd not seen even a glimmer in his eye for years now.

She *had* seen hints of a temper. A hardness in his gaze when she or Mama contradicted him or he didn't get his way. Mama had always been so careful around him, jumping to provide for his every need or whim. Was it out of love…or fear?

He'd never hit either one of them. She would remember if he had.

He'd been…disappointing sometimes. A memory from when she was seven slipped in, pressing on her chest like it always did.

She glanced up at Sampson to see if he was watching her. The one eye not swollen shut rested lightly, and his chest rose and fell in a steady rhythm. Had he fallen asleep? If she spoke aloud, would he hear her? A part of her wanted him to know she really hadn't realized her father was capable of this.

"I'm sorry, Sampson." She spoke the words in a whisper, watching his face for any sign he heard. Or that he was awake.

No change in his features, just that regular rise and fall of his chest. He breathed through his mouth, she guessed because the swelling around his nose didn't allow enough air through.

Fresh tears burned at her eyes. "I'm so, so sorry. I had no idea my father would do something like this. He was never mean to me or Mama. Distant maybe. He came to see us once a month. When I was little, he played with me. I looked forward to his coming so much. Then there was one time, he asked if we wanted to come live with him."

The memory wrapped around her so easily. She'd been sitting on his lap, though she was too old to do so at seven. Mama had been wiping the table, and when Father asked the question, she looked up sharply. So much joy had flooded Grace at the idea, she'd grabbed his arm and asked, *Really? At the mine?*

"He said he was moving to a new house, away from the mine. He said he would come back for us in exactly one week's time. That we should be ready for him. Have all our things packed." She swallowed down the ache in her throat. "I was so excited. I did most of the packing I think, and too early. We had to keep taking dishes and clothing out of the crates to use them before the day came."

She let out a shaky breath. She never allowed herself to relive this. Why was she doing so now? It seemed important somehow. Maybe she could uncover a clue about Father's real nature. Something she should have seen long ago.

"I sat on the front step waiting for him all day. I'd worked it out in my mind that he would probably come around ten o'clock. That would give him enough time to ride to us, and we'd have most of the day to load the wagon and travel to wherever his new house was. I could tell Mama was worried, but I thought it was just concern about whether she'd like our new home. I kept telling her it would be wonderful. That she'd see." What a naive child she'd been. Mama had known. Why hadn't she told her the truth?

A single tear slipped through her defenses, but she ignored it and pushed on. "He never came. I sat on the stoop all day long. Mama kept encouraging me to come away. To go check on the horses or walk down to the creek with her. I wouldn't budge, though, and finally she sat with me. We ate the noon meal there. Then she brought cards, and we played Pinochle and Tuppen. She made my favorite food, berry pancakes, and we ate until we couldn't take another bite. When dark settled, she coaxed me into leaving the doorway." Another tear slipped past. "I think that was the first time I let myself see that he wasn't just busy. He really didn't care about us. Not enough."

She had to sniff but kept the sound quiet.

By the steady rise and fall of Sampson's chest, he was still asleep.

"He proved that over and over through the years. When I was twelve, I got really sick. A fever and casting up accounts. I can't remember what else, just that I thought I was dying. When I opened my eyes, sometimes my vision went dark or fuzzy. Mama was doing everything she could for me, but nothing helped. I begged her to go find Father. To send him for a doctor. I feared…" Her voice broke as emotion swarmed her chest. She sucked in breath after breath.

She had to push on. Had to get this out. "I feared dying and leaving her alone there. I guess, somehow, I knew how awful it would be. To live there in the valley with no one. It's…it's like being the last person on earth. The quiet will make you go mad." Her chest heaved, and she felt as if she couldn't get enough air.

She sucked in breath after breath. She had to stop these memories. Couldn't let herself drown in the grief of missing Mama.

This was about Father. About Sampson.

As she worked to slow her inhales, she forced her mind back to the present. "I never knew Father could be so cruel. I'd never have let him force you into marrying me. I'd never have put you in danger."

But now that she knew the truth, what could she do about it? Would Father come after her here? Would he take his anger out on Sampson again? Or on someone else in the family? These people were so kind. All of them, welcoming her—a stranger—into their midst.

She couldn't let them be hurt. Another glance at Sampson sent a shiver through her. So much damage. So much pain. She couldn't risk anything more.

She and Ruby had to leave here. She had no other choice.

CHAPTER 14

*S*ampson's body ached against the thin mattress as shadows lengthened across the bunkhouse walls. His head hurt less with his eyes closed, so he kept them shut. Grace had left the bunkhouse a while ago, but her strained voice echoed through his mind. He'd nodded off at one point. Then her desperate words had seeped into his awareness gradually, like rainwater finding cracks in a tin roof.

"…so sick…wouldn't let the doctor come."

Or something like that.

The story muddled in his mind, but the pain, the desperation…the loneliness. Those had rung clearly in her voice. They'd seeped into his bones, cracking something deep inside him.

How much pain had this woman endured at the hands of her own father? Jedidiah might not have raised a hand to her the way he did to the men under his thumb, but he'd inflicted a different kind of damage, keeping her and her mother shut away from any comfort or kindness. And after her mother passed, he'd abandoned Grace to grieve alone in that remote house, cut off from anyone who might have offered solace.

And now, she blamed herself for his beating. The thought made his stomach churn.

Jedidiah only acted out of self-interest, and he seemed far more concerned with his lust for the riches and power the mines brought him than with his daughter's welfare. He wouldn't waste effort on punishing Sampson unless he felt a need to assert his authority.

Or to reprimand Sampson for some perceived slight.

Had Sampson questioned where Jedidiah was leading them that night? He knew better than to challenge the man directly. No, the pieces didn't fit. He'd have to untangle this mess later when his head didn't throb so much.

For now, though, he needed to convince Grace that she wasn't to blame for her father's actions. And that she didn't need to leave the ranch. She *couldn't* leave.

Unless she wanted to, of course.

He'd promised her the freedom to choose, after all. Perhaps he needed to honor that, to trust her judgment.

But what if her choice put her in danger?

A low growl of frustration rumbled in his throat, sending fresh shards of pain through his skull.

"Tired of your own company already?"

The unexpected voice made him crack open his good eye. Gil filled the doorway, Miles just behind him.

He'd not even heard the door open.

Gil stepped inside, then Miles.

His brothers. It was so good to see them again. He'd missed them. But that thought came tinged with the bitter taste of failure. He owed them an apology and so much more.

Both men seemed to study his face. Taking in the injuries now that they had daylight, no doubt.

Miles spoke first. "How you feeling?"

If he could have, he would have laughed at the question. Too many ways to answer, but he settled for, "Rough."

Gil leaned against the top bunk. "We're glad to have you back. You're just in time too. Christmas was two days ago, but we decided to put it off until after this mess with McPharland is over. That way we can have a real celebration. Glad you'll be here for it."

Home for Christmas. The idea felt too good to be true. Would he really still be here by then? He had to get back to Jedidiah and finish what he'd started.

"One other change around here too." Miles spoke this time. "We have a new hand, Hiram Pendleton, and his niece, Clara. They came through with a surveying group, but...well, it's a long story, but they ended up staying on."

Something in Miles's tone sounded off, almost protective. And the way he said the woman's name... Sampson focused his eye on his youngest brother. "She the woman I saw with you and Jude in town?"

Miles's cheeks flamed, even more than they had from the cold. He straightened a little. "Yeah."

If that reaction hadn't said enough, the smirk on Gil's face as he eyed Miles made the reality clear.

Sampson let his eye drift shut. "Well, little brother. I guess you're all grown up."

A throat cleared, and Sampson forced his eye open again.

Gil stood with his arms crossed. "Speaking of being grown up, it might be time for you to stay up at the house with your wife and daughter. And closer to the doc. It'd save her the trouble of trekking down here in the cold."

Another pang of guilt twisted his gut. He was being unfair to Dinah. But he couldn't bear the thought of burdening everyone else with his pitiful condition. And he wasn't quite ready to face the whole family. "Better for you all if I'm out of the way."

Miles raised an eyebrow, his expression a mix of disbelief and frustration. "Better for who? You've got a wife and daughter who need you."

Wife and daughter.

The words felt like a jab. What help could he possibly be to Grace like this? Broken and useless. "She needs someone better than me."

Miles crossed the small space to sit on the bunk across from him, right where Grace had settled. He propped his arms on his legs as he leaned forward. "You might be right about that. But you're her husband. Your job now is to *become* the man she needs." His tone sounded like the little brother he'd spent so much time with through the years. Yet somehow wiser.

Gil stepped closer and crouched between the bunks, closing the half-circle they made. "He's right. You've brought her this far. You can't just abandon her when it gets hard. That woman up there, she's hurting. And as many kindhearted females as there are in that house ready to help, they're all strangers to her. I'd bet my last dollar that having you there would make all the difference in the world to Grace right now."

His words bit deep. Too deep.

The stubborn, ornery part of him reared up, ready for a fight. "I'm barely more than a stranger to her myself. Her father forced this marriage on her after I gave her a ride to Missoula and we stayed in that old trapper's cabin overnight. She doesn't want me. I'm just a reminder of everything she's trying to leave behind."

He hated this part of himself. Why couldn't he just give in and agree with them? They were right. Probably. Grace might appreciate having him nearby. A more familiar face. Except... this bruised and swollen version wasn't familiar to either of them.

Miles stretched out his legs, the bunk creaking under the shift of his weight. "So you didn't mean it then? When you vowed before God to love her, to care for her in sickness and health, for better or worse?"

If he'd had the strength, Sampson might've kicked him. Trust Miles to throw those words back at him.

He couldn't even glare properly with one eye. "I meant it. I did that by bringing her here. I'm still doing it by staying away until I'm fit to be what she needs."

Miles leaned forward again, elbows braced on his knees. "Here's the thing. None of us are ever going to be good enough. Not on our own. That's why we need God and each other, why we're stronger together. You can't do this alone, so it's a good thing you came home. Now, are you going to let us help you up to the house, or are you going to hide down here and leave your woman to fend for herself?"

Put like that, it didn't seem he had much of a choice. Grace deserved far better than him, especially now. But since she was stuck with him, he had no choice but to step up and try to be the man she needed, broken pieces and all.

And he could start by not leaving her alone.

~

*G*race sat in the main room near the fire, watching as Jess rested in the rocking chair, feeding Ruby.

They had to leave. She'd made the decision, and she had to carry it out. For Sampson's sake. And his family's. She couldn't risk bringing her father's wrath down on the entire Coulter clan.

But how could she make herself walk away from this place? These people?

So many women eager to help with Ruby. So many arms, sometimes she felt as though she had to beg just to get the chance to cradle her daughter herself.

Her heart ached at the thought of leaving, of taking Ruby away from this warmth and love. The Coulters had welcomed them without question, enfolding them into their family despite

MISTY M. BELLER

the danger and complications. Could she really turn her back on that?

But staying could put them all at risk.

If her father had been so horrible to Sampson because of her, what would he do to the Coulters for helping her? She couldn't let that happen. They'd already sacrificed so much for her sake.

The latch on the front door shifted, and she glanced up as the door opened. A draft of cold air swept in...along with Sampson.

She sucked in a breath as her mind caught up with the unexpected sight. Then her body jolted into action, pushing to her feet.

He hobbled into the room, followed by the two brothers closest in age to him. Gil, the older and Miles, the younger. Miles's shoulders hadn't broadened as much as his older brothers'. For that matter, Sampson seemed more filled out than even Gil, who he'd said had him by a year and a half.

The tingle of pride at her husband's stature faded quickly as her gaze moved up to his face. *Oh, Sampson.* Her heart ached with the pain he'd endured. Was still enduring.

He shuffled a couple steps forward, then halted. Still only one eye could open, but he lifted that eye to meet her gaze. She couldn't tell his expression, not with all the swelling.

She managed a smile of welcome and moved closer. "Are you feeling better?"

"Some." His voice didn't rasp as much as it had earlier. "Thought it was time I stop hiding away."

Grace nodded, but what should she say? Seeing him eased a little of the knot inside her. She wanted to go to him, to wrap her arms around him and give what comfort she could.

But she wasn't the kind of wife who did that, especially not in front of his family. And touching him like that might hurt, considering all his injuries.

He motioned toward the bed chamber. "Is it all right if I take the second bed?"

She glanced toward Jess. Clara slept in the other cot, but she couldn't tell Sampson no. Maybe Grace could sleep on the floor in there.

"Of course it is." Clara herself stepped from the bed chamber, a bright smile on her face and her arms loaded with clothing. "We already discussed it. I'm moving up to the loft with Patsy and Lillian. The only reason I hadn't done it yet was to be close by to help with Ruby during the night."

Grace's throat tightened. "Clara, I can't ask you to give up your bed. I'll take—"

"Nonsense." Clara shook her head. "Your husband needs you close while he heals. It's no trouble at all."

Heat crept up Grace's neck at the implication, however innocent. Had Sampson not told them that their marriage wasn't a true one?

She forced a smile. "If you're sure..." At least this way, she wouldn't have to fight the niggle of jealousy that raised its head at the thought of Clara sleeping in the same room as Grace's husband.

"I am." Clara shifted the bundle of clothing under her arm. "I'll take these up to the loft. Call if you need anything." With a parting smile, she turned to the ladder mounted to the wall by the kitchen.

Grace looked back to Sampson, and the pain etched on his face squeezed her chest once more. Even with the swelling, she could see the determined set of his jaw, the tension in his shoulders as he fought to stay upright.

"Let's get you settled." She led the way into the bed chamber.

He limped behind her, his brothers following. The three men filled the room, shrinking the space. She did her best to focus on Sampson as he eased down to sit on the mattress.

"Does it hurt if I touch this arm?" She rested her fingers on the forearm of the one not broken.

"Naw." Sampson grunted the word, then sucked in a breath as he turned and lifted his feet onto the bed.

Dinah said his ribs were broken, so using those muscles to lie back would be painful.

She plumped the pillow, then braced a hand behind Sampson's shoulders as he eased down. Once he rested on the blankets, he let out a long slow breath and closed his good eye.

He must be exhausted.

"I can bring a cloth packed with snow. That might help with the pain." She started to rise.

But Miles spoke first. "I'll get it."

Grace shook her head. "I can see to it." She needed something to do to help Sampson. "But thank you." She met Miles's gaze, then Gil's, trying to convey her gratitude. "For everything."

Understanding shone in their eyes as both brothers nodded. They eased out of the room, but before she could follow, Sampson touched her arm.

She paused halfway up.

He didn't open his eye as he spoke. "Stay. I don't need ice."

She sank back to the bed, his hand slipping off her arm. "If you're sure."

Her stomach fluttered with nerves, but she pushed them down. Sampson needed her. Or maybe just wanted her here with him. She could sort out the rest later.

"I'm sorry." His voice came out little more than a rasp.

"For what?"

"For..." He lifted his hand, but let it drop back to the quilt as if the effort was too much. "For being a heel. For hiding in the bunkhouse. For not being here to help you like I should."

"You have nothing to apologize for." But the fact that he thought so eased the knot in her middle. He realized he'd left her alone here.

Not that he should be worrying about her when he was in so much pain. If only she could touch him. Maybe smooth the hair back from his brow. "I'm just glad you're here. And getting better." Hopefully. He still looked…

Her eyes watered as she stared at his obvious pain. How many times had the fists hit his face to cause such damage? Were bones broken under the swelling?

A light knock sounded at the door, and Grace turned as Jess poked her head in, Ruby in her arms. "I hope I'm not interrupting. Ruby's wide awake and fussing a bit. I thought she might want to see her papa."

Grace smiled and stood to take the babe as Jess brought her close. "Of course. Come here, sweet girl." She cradled Ruby against her chest as she sank back onto the bed, her daughter's warm weight and soft scent soothing her ragged emotions.

Sampson's good eye opened and fixed on Ruby, and Grace shifted her so the two could see each other better. "There's my girl. Have you been good for your mama?" A ghost of a smile curved his lips.

The babe stared at him, her tiny mouth working.

Grace swallowed a knot of emotion. "She's been an angel, as always. Your sisters-in-law have been wonderful, doing nearly everything for her."

His gaze lifted to Grace and held for a minute. "I'm glad." She still couldn't read his expression. If only she could see more than a sliver of his eye. His tone held…not hesitation, but something more than relief.

He looked back at Ruby and lifted his hand, moving slowly as if each inch cost him a great deal. He reached out, brushing one thick finger against Ruby's tiny hand. The babe latched on, gripping so tight her knuckles turned white.

Sampson's face softened, the lines of pain easing in a small smile.

Ruby's wide blue eyes remained fixed on him, studying his face as if committing every feature to memory.

"She's got quite a grip." Sampson's raspy whisper filled with wonder.

"She does." Grace blinked back the tears that threatened. "She knows her papa."

The words came without thought, but as soon as they left her lips, the truth of them hit her. Ruby had a father now. A good, strong man who would love and protect her. Teach her and guide her.

If she stayed here with him.

How could she ever tear the child away from all this? From the chance to grow up with a devoted father and a large, loving family? It was everything Grace had always yearned for, everything she wanted to give her daughter.

Tears pricked at her eyes. Leaving the Coulters—leaving Sampson—would break her heart, perhaps beyond repair. But staying would put them all in danger, Sampson most of all. Her father would come for her, and his vengeance would be swift and merciless.

She couldn't let that happen. She had to protect Sampson and his family, even if it meant sacrificing her own happiness. Her own heart.

CHAPTER 15

*A*fter he awoke, Sampson lay still with his eyes closed the next morning, taking inventory of his body. The vestiges of sleep still clung to him, but the ache in his left arm, up near the shoulder, wouldn't let him fall back to sleep.

The rest of his body didn't ache nearly as much as it had last night. Maybe he could finally get out of bed without his head splitting. Dinah had said his only broken bones were the arm and a couple ribs.

He opened his eyes, and for the first time since this whole debacle happened, he could actually see a slit of light through the lashes of both. Thank the Lord. The swelling must be lessening. Finally.

For a long minute, he gave his body time to come alive, letting his mind wander back to when he awoke that first morning, shivering under the furs and shelter Two Stones had made for him.

He could remember so much clearer now than in those first minutes. Driving the wagon out of Missoula with Jedidiah riding ahead on his horse. Sampson had hated being gone from Grace all day. And he'd wondered why they were headed east instead of west, to where Jedidiah had him park the blasting powder.

After hours and when darkness had nearly fallen, the man led them off the main road.

The feeling that something wasn't right pressed hard in Sampson's chest. He'd worried about...having a place to turn the wagon around. The path they traveled wasn't a regularly traveled trail, much less a road.

This was more than he'd been able to remember before, but he did his best not to think about that. Not to let his pulse pick up or strain for more. He just let himself rest there, driving through the shadowy woods. Jedidiah's horse ahead of the team.

There had been lights. One glowing that became two. Or... more?

Men.

He remembered the men approaching Jedidiah. Their boss getting off his horse. Standing by the fire. He couldn't hear what they said.

After that, he'd been talking to Jedidiah himself by a fire. Near the stewpot. Something about blasting powder. The mine. Darkness. Maybe because it had been dark at the time?

He could feel the fear in his chest. The realization that what was going to happen would be awful. He had to stop it.

Even now, his heartbeat pounded, and his breath came in shallow gasps. A fear this real... Jedidiah must have been planning to come for their ranch. Right? All those men. They must have been part of it. Joe. And Albert. He could see their faces. See the man with the coonskin cap talking to Jedidiah.

He had to warn his brothers. If Jedidiah was coming for the ranch, he could arrive any time. They had to be ready.

He pushed up to sitting, forcing away the searing in his ribs. The scent of coffee and bacon drifted from the main room, so maybe the men were still here.

After placing his stockinged feet on the floor, he wrapped

his good hand around his ribs and stood. Every muscle protested, some even screaming at him. He held onto the post at the foot of the bed and let himself breathe through the dizziness and pain that threatened to send him right back down.

At last, the room steadied enough for him to let go and shift toward the door. He reached for the handle, and when he took hold, he let himself stop and gather his wits once more.

Then he pulled it open and stepped from the chamber.

His family sat around the table, and all turned to look at him. His focus blurred at a distance, and he couldn't make out individual features.

Dinah's voice sounded first. "Sampson, you shouldn't get out of bed." That must be her moving toward him, a blur coming from the kitchen.

He gripped the doorframe, steadying himself. "I remember." His voice came out in a rasp, but he knew from experience clearing his throat would feel like a gunshot in his skull. "I remember what happened."

Dinah reached his side, her hand grasping his elbow. "You need to rest."

Others had risen from the table and were coming toward him.

He shook his head, regretting the action as pain lanced through his head. "It's Jedidiah." He sucked in a breath, hating his weakness. "He's planning something. An attack on the ranch."

Jericho stopped in front of him and looked like he wanted to reach out. Before he could do, though, another figure, smaller, slipped around him.

Grace.

She didn't hesitate to step close, and Dinah released his elbow as Grace eased herself under his good arm. She fit perfectly there. Small and warm. Just the right height to steady him. He released the door frame and settled his hand on her shoulder.

"Let's sit by the fire." Her voice was gentle. Soft enough to be just for him. "There's room for everyone to listen."

He let her lead him. Let her lower him into the armchair with the tallest back.

When his body sagged into the seat, he rested his head and released a breath. This felt much more manageable than gripping the doorway to keep from swooning.

"Now." Jericho's deep timbre gentled. "Tell us everything you remember."

Most of his brothers had gathered around. Only Jude was missing. He must still be at his cabin down the mountain.

Not even his brothers had scared Grace away though. She perched in the ladderback chair beside him. Close, but not touching.

He needed contact with her. He reached for her hand, and she turned her wrist so their palms met. He wrapped his fingers around hers. A lifeline.

The connection refilled his strength, and he drew in a breath to face his brothers. "I was driving a wagon full of supplies behind Jedidiah. He took me to a camp, deep in the woods between here and Missoula. A bunch of hired men were staying there, rough types." He searched for what else he could remember. "They said something about blasting powder."

"Blasting powder?" Jonah asked sharply, exchanging a look with Jericho. "What would they do with that?"

His brother's question unlocked a memory. "I delivered it."

"What?" Jericho's voice turned sharper.

"The day before. He had me take a wagon of blasting powder out and park it two hours west of Missoula. I thought he was planning a new mine there. But that night I heard him talking to another man. They mentioned blasting powder, and I think my delivery was to throw me off." That sounded just like something Jedidiah would do.

He paused to catch his breath, the pain in his ribs flaring. Grace's fingers tightened around his, lending an extra dose of strength.

"You think the blasting powder is for our mine?" Gil asked.

Another memory surfaced, and he strained to pull it up fully. "I think...they said something about leaving out at first light. Then attacking after dark." He couldn't recall the exact words. Just that general idea.

And thinking so much made his head pound again. He pressed his eyes closed. When the pounding lessened, he opened them.

Jericho's expression had turned grim, his brows lowering. "If they were leaving at first light the next morning, they would have been here two days ago. They would have already attacked."

Two days... Had he been here that long?

"Think the reason they're waiting is the same as why they beat Sam to a bloody mess?" Miles sent him a wary look.

Jonah eyed Sampson. "Why did they beat you? Do you recall the details?"

He let his eyes close as he focused on the scenes in his mind. "The last thing I remember was talking to Jedidiah. Near the stewpot. I was trying to get him to focus on another mine instead of ours." Had he convinced the man? He remembered feeling he might be succeeding in the distraction. "I don't... know."

No other details would come. No words Jedidiah might have said. No memory of the attack. Nothing. His memories just went dark.

He sighed and opened his eyes. "That's the last thing I know for sure. From what I've seen of Jedidiah, my guess is he suspected my loyalties might be divided and chose to cut me from the group." All those months he'd exhausted himself to gain the man's trust...gone in a single conversation.

Jericho spoke again. "Do you think they meant first light the next morning and either chose to delay or were forced to by something? Or do you think they were planning first light of a future day?"

Sampson searched for the memory. "I...I can't be certain. It's all hazy. But I have a sense it was the next morning they planned to head out. Which means something delayed them."

"Maybe gathering more men and weapons took longer than expected." Jericho scrubbed a hand over his stubbled jaw. "Or that snow slowed their progress."

He dropped his hand and turned to Jonah, his gaze taking in Miles and Gil too. "We don't have much time. One of us needs to let Eric know what's happening. And someone should ride for Two Stones, and stop at Jude's on the way. This is probably the time we need to gather the Salish braves he said would come if we needed more manpower against McPharland."

Miles nodded. "I can ride for Jude and Two Stones."

Patsy's voice sounded from behind. "I'll go tell Eric and Naomi. They might need help bringing the children here."

"Good." Jericho nodded. "Best head out now."

When the two had bundled up and slipped out the door, Jericho turned back to Sampson. "Any idea how much blasting powder?"

"At least twenty crates."

Gil let out a low whistle. "That'd blow a decent sized hole in this mountain."

A heavy quiet settled, broken when Jonah spoke. "A couple of us should go see where they are. It makes sense that the snow blocked the trail for a wagon, but they might be moving it a different way now."

"We might be able to disable the powder too," Sampson added. He had to be part of that scouting group, but he had a feeling they'd try to keep him here. Easing the idea into the conversation might help.

"Yes, *we* might." Jericho gave him a pointed look, heading off what he must've guessed Sampson was getting at. "But you'll be staying right here where you can heal."

Not a chance. He had to go. This was his problem to fix. Not even Jericho with all his eldest-brother-in-charge glares could stop him.

He tightened his grip on Grace's hand and met Jericho's gaze squarely. "I'm the only one who knows where their camp is. My memories of the place could be crucial. And I know how Jedidiah works. You need me out there."

Jericho's jaw tightened. "You're in no condition to be traipsing through the mountains, little brother. You can barely ride, much less fight, if it comes to that."

"I don't have to fight. I just have to show you where to go." He held his brother's gaze, willing him to understand. "This is my responsibility. I'm the one who brought this danger to our family."

Jericho stared at him for a long moment, conflict warring in his eyes. Then he lifted his gaze to something—or someone—behind Sampson. Maybe Dinah.

At last, he released a heavy breath, and frustration narrowed his gaze. "Fine. But Dinah will tell you what you can and can't do on the ride, and you'll follow her orders to the smallest bandage."

Sampson might have chuckled if it didn't hurt so much. Even when he was giving in, Jericho just couldn't let go of control. Dinah had a good head on her shoulders. She would be smart about what she required. "Yes, sir."

A snort sounded from one of his brothers.

A glimmer of humor flashed in Jericho's gaze, but then fled as he turned to Jonah and Gil, probably trying to decide who else should go.

Gil spoke in a firm voice. "I'll stay at the ranch and keep watch."

"I guess I'll ride along with you." Jonah slid a half grin toward Sampson. "In case you need an extra hand to get him back in one piece."

Sampson let one side of his mouth tip up. His brothers could tease him all they wanted. This was his fight, and he wouldn't be found missing when the time came to step up.

"All right then." Jericho's commanding voice took charge once more. "We'll get our gear and saddle the horses. Sampson, stay here where it's warm until we come for you."

As his brothers headed out to prepare, the group around him slipped away. Only Grace stayed with him, settled in the chair next to him, her hand in his.

There was so much he needed to say. To explain why he had to go. Did she even know about the mine?

He dared a look at her. Those dark blue eyes were clouded with worry. And maybe uncertainty.

He cleared his throat. "I, um, don't know if I've told you that we have a mine on our property. A sapphire mine. That's what your father's coming after. For McPharland. They came and stole a wagon full of sapphires a few months ago, and now they're coming back for more."

Confusion clouded her gaze, but slowly gave way to shock as her eyes widened. "He stole from you?"

He nodded, but that too-familiar pang twisted in his belly. He shifted his focus forward. "A year's worth of work. But it was my fault. I'm the one who trusted the wrong men. I practically led them here." He took in a breath to steady himself. "That's why I have to go, to fix this."

"Sampson." That single word sounded half-reproving, half-anxious.

What was she worried about exactly? For him? Or for her father's safety?

Or maybe she feared that if something happened to Sampson, she and Ruby would be turned out with nothing to live on. No way for a fresh start.

He rubbed his thumb across the back of her hand. They'd not held hands before, but now that he knew the feel of her, he couldn't get enough.

He kept his voice low enough that the women working in the kitchen wouldn't hear. "Are you worried?"

"Of course I am. You're in no condition to leave this house, much less ride for hours in the cold. And what if my father sees you? What else would he do to you?"

So not worried about her father's well-being. He gave her hand a little squeeze. "You don't need to be concerned. If something happens and I don't come back, my family is still your family. You'll always have a place here, if you want it. And you'll have my full share of the mine and ranch." He swallowed past the lump in his throat. "You and Ruby won't ever want for money."

Her eyes had widened, the concern turning to something like fear. "Sampson, no." She gripped his wrist with her other hand. "You can't go. Not if you think you might not make it back."

He didn't have a free hand, not with his lame arm strapped to his side. So he squeezed Grace's to add a bit of reassurance to his words. "That's not what I meant. Sorry, I was just trying to ease your mind."

Red rimmed her eyes now, and he could smack himself for such careless words. "Grace, I promise. I'll be fine. You don't have to worry."

She dropped her gaze to their joined hands, and a single tear trailed down her cheek. His chest ached, a much deeper pain than the cracked ribs.

"I'm sorry, Grace." He needed her to look at him. To read the truth in his eyes. Gently, he extracted his hand from hers and lifted his palm to cradle her cheek, using his thumb to wipe away the trail of moisture.

Finally, she looked at him, and the pain in those beautiful blue orbs nearly undid him.

"I have to do this." He kept his voice gentle, though he wanted her to understand how important this was to him. "I'm the one who got our family into this mess, and I need to be part of getting us out of it. But I promise I will come back to you and Ruby. I'm not leaving you alone. You have my word."

"You can't promise that, Sampson. No one can. If my father would do this to you...." Her voice broke, and she dropped her gaze again.

The vulnerability in her tone ripped at his heart. He traced his thumb over her cheekbone. "You won't lose me. Jericho and Jonah will watch my back. We're just going to scout things out and make a plan. I'll be safe as can be."

She gave a small nod, though she still didn't look at him. "Just...be careful. Please."

"I will. I promise." *God, am I making the wrong decision?*

But he had to go. He knew Jedidiah's ways better than any of them. He had to be the one to make this right.

After a long moment, she released a shaky breath and straightened, pulling her hand from his. "I'll help Dinah pack what you'll need."

He watched her go, praying he'd be able to keep his promise to her.

CHAPTER 16

*G*race paced in front of the stone fireplace, her footsteps muffled by the woven rug. Ruby squirmed in her arms, fussing against the swaddling blanket. She clutched the babe tighter, murmuring soothing words even as her own heart raced with worry.

Most of the women and children had gone to the bunkhouse, but Jess stayed here in the main cabin with her, sewing in the rocking chair while Grace fretted.

Sampson had been in no condition to leave. He'd barely been able to walk across the room, much less ride a horse. And up against her father and a camp full of hired ruffians...

She shouldn't have let him go.

Learning about what her father had already done to the Coulters, stealing so much from them, made her furious. How dare he hurt such good people? Even if it was at McPharland's command.

If she had a chance to reason with her father, maybe she could make him stop this madness. Make him realize how much damage he'd already done.

"Would you like me to rock her?" Jess studied Grace, her brow wrinkled.

Grace sighed and shook her head. "She's probably picking up on my worries."

She refocused on Ruby and bounced a little as she slowed her pacing. "It's all right, my love. Everything will be all right."

Ruby quieted, resting her sweet head on Grace's shoulder.

Grace eased out a long, slow breath. She couldn't let her tension affect Ruby so.

"Are you worried about Sampson's injuries?" Jess's voice held a hesitant tone. She was quieter than the other women, but that made it almost easier to be around her. It was hard to believe their fathers had worked together. That Jess had lived only a couple hours' ride from her all those lonely years.

Grace met the woman's perceptive blue eyes. "Yes. And about what my father will do." Should she say the rest? Maybe she could test the idea on Jess. "I wish I could talk to my father. I might be able to stop him." Jess seemed to be considering the idea, so Grace pressed on. "I think I need to ride after them. Maybe I can end all this before someone else gets hurt." Hurt worse than Sampson had already suffered.

Jess's eyes widened and she lowered her sewing. "Grace, I don't think you're the reason your father is coming." She paused, her lips rolling in. "It's no secret my father wants the Coulters' land, and he's ordered your father to take it for him. Papa's greed is driving all of this."

Grace swallowed past the lump in her throat.

Jess might be right. But she couldn't shake the conviction that she was the spark that had ignited this powder keg.

And she might be the only one who could stop the explosion.

She shook her head, her choice hardening into resolve. "I understand that, Jess. But I'm sure my presence here is making things worse. If I can intercept my father, appeal to him, maybe I can stop this before it goes any further."

Grace met Jess's concerned gaze. "Will you watch over Ruby for me? I'll ride fast and catch up to them."

Jess hesitated. After a long moment, she sighed and rose from the rocking chair. "Of course I'll care for Ruby. But Grace, please be careful. Your father...he's not a reasonable man."

"I know." Grace's voice caught. "But I have to try. For Sampson…and for all of you."

Jess took the babe from her arms. "Let's go tell the others. I have a feeling you won't be going alone."

Half an hour later, Grace stood in the yard and pressed a final kiss to Ruby's soft brow. "Be good for Aunt Jess and the others. Mama will be back as soon as I can."

Sampson's family had indeed protested her plan, but they hadn't forced her to stay. Thankfully, Miles returned around that time with Two Stones and three other braves. Two Stones told the group that his cousin had gone to gather the rest of the braves from their village and another nearby camp. They'd be here by morning.

For now, she would ride with Two Stones and his companions to catch up with Sampson and his two oldest brothers. She would never admit how much relief she felt to be traveling with Two Stones instead of by herself, especially since they would likely ride after dark.

She couldn't delay this parting any longer. As she eased the babe back into Jess's waiting arms, tears blurred her vision, and she turned away to hide them.

She couldn't bring herself to meet the gazes of the Coulter family who stood with Jess. They would surely try again to talk her out of going. She'd already received farewell hugs from Dinah and Patsy and Naomi and Clara and Angela and Jess and even Lillian, Sampson's niece. So many women who'd become her family, at least in name. She'd gone from desperately lonely to overwhelmed with kin in just a few days.

Would she have to lose them all soon? She would do her very best to keep that from happening.

She swung aboard the bay mare she'd ridden that first time when Two Stones brought her to the ranch. This mission felt so much more frightening than that other.

She managed a glance at the Coulters. "Thank you, all. For everything." Her voice cracked, and she swallowed down the emotion. "I'll be back as soon as I can."

She turned her mare toward the four men waiting. Two Stones raised a hand in farewell to the Coulters, then nudged his horse forward.

She moved her horse in line with the others, the knot in her stomach tightening with each of the animal's strides. What would she say to her father when she found him? Could she truly persuade him to call off this attack?

She had to. For Sampson. For Ruby. For...everyone.

～

Sampson's body throbbed with his horse's every movement. Dinah had sent medicine for the pain, as well as a flask of tea he'd been sipping on, but he'd asked for smaller doses so he could stay alert.

The lesser amount definitely didn't help as much, but he could stay awake. He still couldn't move without sharp pains shooting through his chest and shoulder. Not to mention the steady ache in his head.

They'd been plodding along for hours now, and he'd allowed Jericho to lead. They planned to go back to the place where Two Stones had set up camp after rescuing Sampson from the beating. From there they would search for Jedidiah's camp on foot, without the horses making so much noise.

Surely, they'd reach that spot soon. Dusk had already fallen, and darkness would be on them in no time. His brothers likely would have moved faster without him, but he couldn't manage the bounce of a trot or canter. As much as he hated to admit it even to himself, that agony might have done him in.

Ahead, Jericho's horse halted, and Jonah reined in beside him. Sampson pulled up, too, biting back a groan as the effort jarred his injuries. He focused on breathing through his nose, willing the pain to subside.

His brothers had already dismounted by the time he managed to ease himself down from the saddle.

Jericho came to his side and took his reins. "Why don't you stay here with the horses? Let yourself rest a while." He kept his voice low, but the tone was far gentler than his usual to-the-point manner.

Shaking his head would hurt too much, so he focused on words. "I'm coming. I'm all right."

The boldest lie he'd ever told, and Jericho knew that too. But he couldn't admit to anything else. He had to say it to keep himself going.

Jericho studied him for a long moment, his brow furrowed. He finally nodded. "All right. You can stop anytime. Jonah and I can scout ahead."

They made their way through the shadowed trees, the snow crunching softly beneath their boots. The icy air bit at his exposed skin, but it also helped numb the relentless throbbing of his injuries.

Small mercies.

At last, Jericho raised a hand for them to stop. He touched his ear, a signal to listen.

Sampson strained to catch any sound. The pounding in his head made it hard to hear much else. Then, faintly, he caught the murmur of voices.

His pulse quickened. They were close.

Jericho motioned them forward, and they crept on, single-file and staying close to the trees. After a few more strides, Jericho halted behind a cluster of several brushy cedars. He waved for them to join him there.

As Sampson crowded close to his brothers, he peered through the branches. Light glowed about twenty strides ahead. The voices sounded louder now, but not loud enough to make out words.

Jericho spoke in the quietest of whispers. "Need to get closer, but we should come in from different sides. One's easier to hide than three."

Jonah pointed to the left. "I'll circle that way and look for cover."

Jericho glanced at Sampson, then pointed ahead on the route they'd been taking. "You should see better from there."

Sampson squinted to make out the spot in the darkness. Another cluster of low cedars beside a taller pine. "Fine." He could manage a whisper easier than a nod at this point.

Jericho motioned to the right. "I'll go that way." He turned back to them both. "Look and listen, but don't get caught. Meet back here in an hour."

Sampson didn't try to answer. After his brothers faded into the darkness, he focused on the spot that would be his aim. The camp was too far away for him to worry overmuch about being caught on his way there, but he should still stay close to trees.

He crept forward, measuring each step as he moved from trunk to trunk. His boots sank into the snow, slowing him. His breath puffed out in white clouds, mingling with the icy air that numbed his face and hands.

As he came closer to the cluster of cedars Jericho had pointed out, the voices from the camp grew louder. He strained to make out words, but the pulsing in his head and the distance still made it difficult.

At last he reached his goal. Letting out a slow breath, he

eased himself against the pine trunk, bracing a hand on the rough bark. Black spots danced in his vision, but he blinked them away. He had to focus.

Peering through the screen of branches, he could make out the flicker of campfires. Dark shapes moved around them. The men's voices carried better here. A bunch of them, all speaking quietly. A few tones rose louder than the rest. This would take time to distinguish the speakers.

He allowed himself to ease down to sit in the snow, resting his shoulder against the trunk so he could peer through the cedar needles as he listened.

That deep voice sounded familiar. Maybe one of the guards. The name eluded him, blocked by his haze of pain.

Then a voice he knew all too well cut through the murmurs, sending a chill down his spine.

McPharland. The big boss himself, the one even Jedidiah had to obey.

When had he come? Maybe that's why Jedidiah had held off the attack.

Sampson leaned forward, straining to catch the words being spoken. McPharland said something about moving the blasting powder.

And then...was that Jedidiah's voice? That calm, menacing tone.

He shifted, trying to get a better view through the cedar branches. A sharp burn stabbed his ribs so hard his lungs stopped. He forced himself to breathe through the agony, shallow and steady.

He had to keep listening too. He couldn't miss a word.

With his eyes shut against the pain, he strained to pick out Mick's or Jedidiah's voices from the others. To decipher their words.

But then, a closer sound pricked his awareness.

Footsteps, crunching in the snow. And coming straight toward him.

He pressed himself back against the pine trunk. Maybe the shadows would conceal him. His heart pounded his aching ribs as the footsteps drew nearer, louder.

He held himself utterly still, not even blinking, as he made out a dark figure through the cedar needles—just a few steps away. The man paused, his head turning to scan the area.

Please, God, don't let him see me.

The man's gaze swept the shadows, and Sampson held his breath, willing himself to melt into the darkness. His heart hammered against his ribs, each beat sending a fresh wave of agony through his battered body.

Please, keep moving. Nothing to see here.

But the man took a step closer, his hand dropping to the pistol at his hip. Sampson's pulse roared in his ears, drowning out the voices from the camp. He couldn't fight, not in this condition. And he couldn't run.

The cedar branches rustled as the man pushed them aside, leaning in to peer at Sampson's hiding spot. In the faint light filtering through the trees, Sampson caught the glint of cold eyes fixed on him.

"Well now." A slow grin spread across his face. "What have we here?"

CHAPTER 17

*a*gony burned through Sampson as he stumbled into the camp, his captor dragging him in an iron grip. The man clutched his good arm, thank the Lord, but still the jolting seared through his body. Black spots danced around his vision as he struggled to keep up.

At last, the stranger halted, though his hold on Sampson's arm tightened like a vise.

He struggled to take in enough air to clear his focus. To see where he was.

"What is this?" Jedidiah's voice blazed with barely concealed fury. "Where did *he* come from?"

The captor jerked Sampson forward a step. "Found him skulking outside camp. Thought you might like to know it."

"I thought he was dead." McPharland's voice held that eerie coldness Sampson had heard too many times.

Sampson strained to focus enough to see the man.

McPharland looked to Jedidiah, and his tone turned almost teasing. "You told me you'd had him killed, did you not?"

"I did."

Sampson had never heard Jedidiah defensive. Never heard

the two men at odds with each other. But Jedidiah looked almost cornered.

And when cornered weasels turned desperate, they usually lashed out.

"Albert!" His roar made Sampson's captor jump, as well as the guard he called.

Albert and Joe both appeared at the edge of Sampson's vision. They were the man's usual henchman and must have been the ones ordered to kill Sampson. The thought fueled the anger in his gut. Jedidiah had actually tried to *kill* him. Only by God's mercy was he still alive today.

For now, anyway.

Maybe kept alive to stop him. To stop both of these mole rats.

"You incompetent fools!" Jedidiah snarled at the guards. "I told you to kill him. Finish the job now, here in front of me."

Both men moved to obey.

"Hold on just a minute." McPharland's voice halted them. He spoke in a smooth drawl. Relaxed and fully in control.

He sauntered over, dark eyes appraising Sampson like a prize horse. "We might still have use for this one. A tool, maybe. Or bait. One never knows."

Jedidiah's face twisted in a sneer. "He's a liability. Best to put him down now."

"Is that any way to treat your son-in-law?" Mick gave Jedidiah a chiding look. He spoke with that same mild tone, yet steel lurked beneath.

Did he disagree with the marriage Jedidiah had forced them into? Probably. There certainly seemed an undercurrent of disagreement between the two of them. Something he'd never heard before.

Usually, they were united in their evil, a fact that made them even more lethal. A rip in the fabric might prove helpful.

Jedidiah's jaw clenched, his eyes narrowing as he met Mick's gaze. For a moment, it seemed he might argue, but then he gave a curt nod. "Fine. Tie him up at the edge of camp. But if he causes any trouble, it's on your head." His voice hummed with barely restrained anger.

Mick just smiled, a cold, calculating curve of his lips. "Of course. I'll take full responsibility."

Joe grabbed Sampson's left elbow—the broken arm still strapped against his chest.

Sampson bit hard on his lip to keep from howling from the fire blazing through him. He stumbled forward, anything to keep the man from jerking him. Flashes of light exploded in his vision.

At last, he was spun around and pressed down to sit on the ground. His head thunked against the hard bark of a tree behind him. He focused on drawing air in, then forcing the breath back out. Past his aching ribs. More air in. Maybe he should let himself pass out. A blessed oblivion from this torture.

But something inside wouldn't give in.

As the men cut loose the bindings Dinah had so carefully wrapped around his arm to secure the bone in place, he worked to keep each breath steady.

Mick's and Jed's voices drifted to him, filtering through the haze of his breathing. He shifted his focus to hear what they were saying, but they spoke too low to make out. He strained harder, yet the words remained elusive. Were they talking about him? About attacking the ranch? He couldn't tell.

One of the guards wrenched the wrist of his broken arm backward. A blaze of agony exploded inside him. He couldn't keep in the cry as he jerked forward.

The man spared him nothing as he forced his wrist down to meet the other.

Sampson jerked in breaths, fighting for control of himself. Fighting for relief from the torment. He needed that oblivion. Now.

Even as his body cried out for relief, a thought crept in.

Jericho and Jonah were out there somewhere. They might try to rescue him. They wouldn't succeed.

They'd be captured too. Or worse. He couldn't let that happen.

He had to find a way out of this mess. On his own. Before someone he loved got hurt.

~

*T*he night pressed in around Grace as she rode, a heavy cloak of darkness broken only by the fleeting glow of stars through the branches overhead. She gripped her reins as her mare picked its way down the steep wooded slope, following the shadowy forms of Two Stones and Sitting Bear. The other two braves rode behind her, hemming her in like a protected child.

She was beyond grateful.

The men had spoken little on this long uncomfortable ride, but Two Stones said they would go first to the camp he'd made to nurse Sampson after he found him so badly beaten. Jericho knew the location of that camp, so he might have also ridden there to begin the search for her father.

A horse nickered in the darkness ahead. Grace's pulse leaped into a gallop. Could it be Jericho and the others, with news of Sampson? Or had they stumbled on her father's camp?

Two Stones held up a hand, signaling the group to halt. He dismounted, then crept forward to investigate.

Grace's breath caught in her throat, her body tense as a drawn bowstring. She strained for any sign of danger, but the night remained still save for the hush of wind through the trees.

Long moments passed before Two Stones returned and motioned them forward. She eased out a breath. That must have been one of the Coulters' horses.

Had he seen Sampson and his brothers?

She nudged her mare forward behind Sitting Bear's horse as they descended the final slope and reached level ground.

Tethered at the edge of a small clearing were several horses she recognized—Sampson's big gray, Jonah's bay, and the paint horse Jericho rode. But no sign of the men themselves.

Two Stones tied his horse near the others, and she moved with the rest of the men to do the same. He stepped close enough that they could all hear his quiet words. "I will go ahead to where I found Sampson. Wait here." He melted into the shadows without a sound.

Grace's hands trembled as she finished tying her reins to the branch. Even with these warm fur-lined gloves Dinah had sent with her, her fingers had numbed hours ago.

After rubbing her mare a few moments, she moved to a place she could better see Two Stones the moment he returned.

The night closed in, thick and oppressive. She fought the urge to pace, to call out, to do anything other than wait in tense silence.

An owl hooted in the distance, the eerie sound sending a shiver down her spine. She'd spent countless nights outside in the wilderness near their home in the valley, but this felt different. Danger crackled in the air like lightning before a storm.

After what felt like an eternity, the crunch of footsteps sounded from the direction Two Stones had gone. Grace straightened, heart in her throat, as a figure materialized from the darkness. Then another.

Jericho and Jonah.

Two Stones followed them, and her chest tightened until she couldn't breathe.

"Where is he?" The words tore from her, raw and desperate. "Where's Sampson?"

Jericho held up a hand, his face hard in the moonlight. "They found him. Brought him into their camp."

"He's tied to a tree." Jonah's voice burned low and tight. "We're waiting for the others to fall asleep before we try to get him out."

"How many?" Two Stones asked.

"About thirty," Jericho said. "All armed."

Thirty men. Thirty guns. And Sampson helpless in their midst. Bile rose in her throat as visions of him broken and bleeding flashed through her mind. She squeezed her eyes shut, willing the images away. She had to stop this.

Then she forced her eyes open and met Jericho's stare head-on. "I need to talk to my father. I have to try to stop this."

Something flickered in his eyes, a brief flash of empathy. "I understand, Grace. But from everything I've heard about Jedidiah and McPharland, I'm not sure their minds can be changed. At least not without coming up against a hard wall."

She opened her mouth to protest, but he held up a hand, forestalling her. "McPharland is dead set on having our mine. Even if Jedidiah wanted to stop, I don't think he could. Not with McPharland pushing him."

The truth of his words settled like a stone in her gut. Her father had chosen his path long ago, and it led them all to this dark precipice. Changing course now seemed as impossible as changing the direction of a river at spring thaw.

But still, the need to do something, anything, pulsed through her. She couldn't stand here waiting while Sampson's life hung in the balance. "Then what can we do?" The question burst out, tinged with desperation. "How do we get him out?"

Jericho exchanged a grim look with Jonah before glancing around at the other men. "We have a plan. It's risky, but I think it's the only way. With six of us, we can spread out around the camp. Wait until they're all asleep, then take out the guards quietly. Get to Sampson and cut him loose before anyone realizes what's happening."

Grace's pulse hammered. It sounded so dangerous. So much could go wrong. But what choice did they have?

She met Jericho's piercing blue gaze. "What do you need me to do?"

His brows lowered. "Grace, I can't let you anywhere near—"

"I have to help." Her voice cracked with emotion. "Please. I can't just sit here. Not when Sampson..." She couldn't finish. The thought of him at her father's mercy made bile rise in her middle.

Jericho sighed, rubbing a hand over his stubbled jaw. "Sampson would have my hide if I let anything happen to you."

"And I'll never forgive myself if I don't help him." Grace lifted her chin, holding his stare. Willing him to understand.

A long moment stretched between them.

"I have a job for you." Two Stones's voice pierced the silence. When she glanced over at him, the way one corner of his mouth tipped up made her heart pick up speed.

"All right." She gave a firm nod. "Tell me what to do."

CHAPTER 18

*S*ampson tucked his chin and curled into himself as much as he could with his arms tied behind him. His body trembled from the cold seeping into his bones. Pain radiated from his shoulder and ribs, a relentless throbbing he couldn't escape.

One of the guards had tossed a blanket on him earlier, but he had no way to spread it, so the fabric pooled on his lap.

He squeezed his eyes shut. There was no way to escape this misery. What he wouldn't give for a full dose of Dinah's laudanum to numb the agony. Or better yet, to be back in the warmth and safety of his family's cabin, with Grace at his side.

He could almost feel her small hand in his as they sat near the fire, her gentle touch soothing away the hurt. Even better, to have her curled up next to him under the quilts, her soft curves fitted against him, chasing away the bitter cold. The mere thought of her brought a flicker of warmth to his chest, a tiny respite from this relentless torment.

Around him, the camp had fallen silent. Some of the men pitched tents to keep out the wind and moisture. Others bedded down under furs closer to the fires. A few snores drifted through the darkness, mingling with the crackling of flames.

The four guards on watch stood or sat around the edges of the clearing. The man closest to Sampson was a fellow he'd never met. Roy, someone had called him. He sat on a tall stump near one of the fires, his back to the flame, facing the darkness with his rifle at the ready. He wore leathers and a fur hat like a man familiar with this country.

Every so often, he glanced Sampson's way. He didn't seem worried about him escaping. Sampson must look half dead, which was exactly the way he felt. How was he going to make it through the night like this, let alone find a way to get free and return to Grace and his family?

Were Jericho and Jonah out there watching? Surely, they wouldn't try to rescue him. They'd be foolish to, with so many armed men here.

An icy wind swept over him, and he curled tighter, trying to conserve what little warmth he had left. The ropes bit into his wrists, the pain a sharp counterpoint to the throbbing ache of his injuries. He shifted, trying to find a more comfortable position, but there was no relief anywhere. His feet had gone numb, and he couldn't feel his fingers.

How in the starry night sky could he possibly get free of this place? Even if he could cut himself loose and the guard turned a blind eye, he wouldn't be able to stand and walk. He would die here, at the hands of these men. McPharland and Jedidiah...his father-in-law.

Grace. What would happen to her and Ruby? His family would take care of them. At least he'd done that right—bringing his wife and daughter to safety on the ranch.

He'd probably never see them again. A burn pressed in his chest, as strong as the ache in his broken arm. Grace's face slipped in. So pretty, with those blue eyes and the quiet smile that made her glow from within. So beautiful. He'd never felt such longing. A yearning so big it stopped his breathing. What he wouldn't give to see her. To hold her.

He'd been a blame fool to agree to a marriage in name only. Not when she stirred every part of him. He should have asked if he could court her. He should have at least told her how much she was coming to mean to him in such a short time.

Now, he'd never have the chance.

He squeezed his eyes shut against the pain. He could do nothing more. Breaking free of this misery would take a power much stronger than him.

A Power even stronger than his brothers.

A new pressure weighed inside him. He'd tried so hard to fix this entire debacle himself. *He'd* been the one to choose the wrong men to trust in the first place. That error had led McPharland's men to his family's mine, and they'd lost a year's worth of earnings.

Maybe if he'd asked God for wisdom that first day in Missoula Mills, he'd not be in this situation. But by the time he realized his error, he'd thought he was in too deep for anyone to fix his mistakes except him.

Foolish, prideful man.

I'm sorry, God. I've messed up. More than can be fixed maybe. But if there's a chance You can get us out of this, please save my family. Keep Grace and the baby safe. Everyone. And if You see fit, save my sorry hide too. Give me another chance with Grace. Show me how to be a real husband to her. The man she needs.

Tears burned his eyes, clumping as ice on his lashes. A second chance felt far too generous for a man who'd failed this miserably.

He opened his eyes and took in a breath, letting his head rest against the tree. He had no control of the situation anymore—if he'd ever had any to start with. Since the pain and cold wouldn't let him sleep, he could spend the rest of his time praying for those he loved.

Thank You for Grace. For bringing her into my life. For the treasure she—

Something shifted in the shadows outside of camp. He squinted to study the spot without making his attention obvious.

It was probably nothing. The moon drifting behind the clouds.

A dark shape moved again, low to the ground, sliding between the trunks of the pines. Not a cloud. A man. He melted into the trees and disappeared.

Sampson's heart hammered. It must be one of his brothers.

Jericho and Jonah might be foolish enough to attempt a rescue, but if they were caught…he couldn't bear the thought of them ending up like him. Or worse.

The figure slipped closer, and Sampson caught a glimpse of the man's profile in the moonlight. Two Stones. Relief flooded through him, followed by a surge of fear. If Two Stones was caught, he'd be killed for sure.

A noise sounded across camp, and Sampson jerked his focus that direction. The guard did too.

Two Stones slipped from the trees, gliding like a silent shadow to Sampson, moving behind the trunk he was tied to.

The guard must have decided the sound was nothing, for he turned back and scanned the tree line, then looked to Sampson.

He did his very best to act natural. Exhausted.

Not like his entire body hummed with energy. Something tugged his wrists, sending a shot of pain up his arm. Then his hands dropped an inch. Was he free? He couldn't tell with so little feeling in his limbs. Even if he was, he would have trouble walking.

The guard still watched him, eyes narrowed, his gaze piercing through the dim light from the fire.

Sampson held his breath, willing himself to remain still despite the agony that wracked his body. The seconds stretched into an eternity as the guard scrutinized him, searching for any sign of deceit.

Just as it looked like the man would come to check him, a commotion erupted on the far side of the camp.

Shouts rang out.

The guard spun, his rifle at the ready, and dashed towards the disturbance.

In a flash, Two Stones crouched at Sampson's side, his knife slicing through the ropes that bound his ankles. "Can you stand?"

He didn't wait for an answer as all around them, men stumbled from their bedrolls, grabbing for weapons.

Two Stones hauled him up, draping Sampson over his shoulder like a sack of flour.

Pain lanced through him, but he clenched his jaw to keep back his cries. Hanging upside down like this, darkness pressed in, peppering his vision.

He couldn't lose consciousness. He had to help. Not be a burden.

With every jolting step Two Stones took, a fresh shot of agony slammed through his battered body. He clung to consciousness, fighting the black that threatened to pull him under.

Shouts and gunshots echoed behind them. Were they getting louder? Was that a woman yelling?

He could feel more than hear Two Stones call out, though he couldn't make sense of the words.

Then Sampson was being shifted. Heaved upright and lifted. Other hands grabbed him, wrapping around his middle.

The darkness... He couldn't tell if it was the night that made it so hard to see or his fading senses. The shouts still sounded, but he couldn't distinguish whether they were distant or close around him. Everything felt distant. Like he'd already slipped halfway to unconsciousness.

At least he was sitting upright now. In a saddle maybe. Arms gripped tight around his belly.

He could only slump against whoever held him.

Then the horse beneath him surged forward. The jolt sent a fresh wave of fire through his shoulder, drawing him back to the present.

Branches scratched at his arms and face as they rode, but scrapes weren't even a nuisance compared to the agony inside him.

"Hold on, Sampson. Please, just hold on."

The voice seemed to come from a great distance, barely audible over the roaring in his ears. But something about it tugged at his memory, a lifeline in the darkness.

Grace. It sounded like Grace.

But that was impossible. Grace was safe back at the cabin with Ruby. With the rest of his family. Surely she wasn't risking her life to save his sorry hide. This had to be a dream, some cruel trick of his mind in his final moments.

A sharp jolt sent fresh agony searing through his body, and he could have laughed at the irony. He wouldn't have thought a dream could be so painful, so viscerally real.

Darkness crept in at the edges of his vision again. The arms around him tightened, anchoring him to the present.

"Stay with me, Sampson. Don't you dare leave us now."

The desperate plea followed him down into the waiting blackness. As much as he wanted to cling to Grace's voice, he no longer had control.

Of anything.

CHAPTER 19

*G*race urged the horse onward in the darkness, her arms aching from hours of holding Sampson's limp form upright in the saddle. His head lolled back against her shoulder, his breathing shallow and ragged in the icy mountain air.

Ahead of her Sitting Bear, the man Two Stones had assigned to guide her back to the Coulter ranch, led the way through the darkness. The others had stayed behind to slow the enemy down. Every few minutes the bang of gunfire sounded. Farther back, but not nearly far enough.

The dark silhouettes of pine branches overhead almost concealed the barely lightening sky. Morning. They'd almost made it through the night. Surely, they couldn't be far from the ranch now.

She tightened her hold around Sampson's waist and spoke into his ear the same thing she'd said so many times through this interminably long ride. "Stay with me, Sampson. We're almost there. Just hold on a little longer."

His only response was a low moan, the words garbled and dreamlike. "Jed...McPharland...mine..."

Her heart ached at the pain in Sampson's voice, even in his delirium. Her father had done this to him. And now his brothers and good friends were still in danger, risking their lives because of her father. It seemed impossible. Yet was all too true.

God, protect them. The Coulter men, the braves. And Sampson. Don't let me lose him. Please.

Sometime in the night she'd started praying to the God Sampson said was real. A desperate act, but it felt worth trying. Sending up those words, even in her mind, had seemed to do something. She'd felt...reassured.

Maybe she only imagined the feeling. Her frantic mind grasping for something—anything—to help this man who might be dying in her arms.

She'd kept up the praying. And each urgent request left a tiny bit of relief in her chest.

Sampson still lived. Was that God answering her prayer? She had no idea, but she didn't intend to stop.

Ahead of her, Sitting Bear reined his horse to an abrupt halt. She did the same.

He pointed up the slope to their left. "Ride to big rock. Find path to Coulter lodge." His voice turned low and urgent. "I go back. Help brothers fight."

Grace squinted through the gray light of dawn, barely making out the boulder he'd pointed to partway up the mountainside. She nodded. "Thank you. For everything."

The brave inclined his head, then turned his horse and pushed the animal into a run past her. Riding toward the fight.

She swallowed the tightness in her throat. So many risking their lives because of her desperate choices. Her arms trembled with fatigue as she shifted Sampson's dead weight, pressing her palm to his chest. His heartbeat thrummed beneath her fingers, rapid but strong.

"We're nearly there." She worked to strengthen her voice. "Stay with me, Sampson."

She nudged her weary mare forward, up the slope Sitting Bear had indicated. When they reached the large rock, a worn trail ran diagonally. She turned right to follow the path upward and the same general direction they'd been riding for hours.

Soon, she should reach the clearing. And the house. And help for Sampson.

Heat too. What she wouldn't give for a hot fire, something to warm her bones so she could feel her limbs again.

The trail wound higher, the brightening sky revealing more of the rugged terrain with each passing minute. Grace's thighs burned from gripping the horse's sides, her muscles stiff and aching. She focused on the rhythm of the mare's hooves against the rocky ground, anything to keep her mind from the exhaustion weighing her body.

At last, the path crested a rise and the trees thinned. The cabin came into view as her mare entered the clearing. Smoke curled from the stone chimney, a promise of warmth and comfort within. And help. Tears stung her eyes.

The front door banged open, and people spilled out. Jude first, then Miles and Gil and a host of others. The entire family maybe.

She reined in when she reached them, and Jude stepped close to take Sampson. "What happened?"

Without his weight to hold up, her body sagged, nearly as limp as Sampson's. "He was caught. They had him tied to a tree. I don't know if they hurt him worse, but he's been mostly unconscious on the ride."

Gil held her horse while Eric reached up to help her down. Jude and Miles were already carrying Sampson into the house, Dinah following closely.

"Where are the others?" Eric asked as she accepted his offer and leaned on his shoulder to slide from the saddle.

She wasn't certain her legs would hold her up when she hit the ground.

He steadied her with a hand on her upper arm. "You all right?"

"They're fighting. Trying to keep my father's men from the house, I think." Her ankles buckled in the snow, and she gripped Eric's shoulder hard to keep from going down.

Naomi slipped herself under Grace's other shoulder. "Come in and get warm while you tell us everything." She wrapped an arm tight around Grace's waist.

Supported between the two of them, she hobbled to the door and up the step. The heat inside swept over her, making her bones go weak once more.

"Sit by the fire." Patsy motioned to the rocking chair. "Ruby's still asleep."

Guilt pressed in as she sat. She'd barely thought of her daughter through those long night hours. Getting Sampson home alive had been her focus. Now, she managed a "Thank you."

"What happened?" Eric asked as Jude and Miles emerged from the bed chamber where they must have laid Sampson. "We'll ride out and help them, but it'd be good to know what we're walking into."

Grace tried to order her scattered thoughts. "We rode to the camp where Two Stones had taken Sampson. Jonah and Jericho met us there and said Sampson had been caught."

"So they're all right? Jonah? And Jericho?" Patsy's voice broke in.

She glanced up at the woman, who stood with Angela, a little behind the men. The hope, the tentative relief on her face pressed in Grace's chest. She'd not even thought about them worrying about the other men. Patsy was Jonah's intended, and their wedding was to happen in a matter of weeks.

She gave an apologetic smile. "Last I saw them, Jonah and Jericho were well. Worried and angry. But not hurt."

Patsy gave a small nod, but her lips rolled in as though she might cry. Poor woman.

"How many men are in the camp? How did you get Sampson free?" Jude's questions drew her back to her retelling.

She finished her story, being as thorough as she could. There wasn't much to tell though. She'd only glimpsed the campfires through the branches from where Two Stones told her to wait, mounted and ready to ride any second. The other men had tied their horses nearby. They'd hoped to all escape quietly once Two Stones freed Sampson, but that first shout had told her the plan went awry.

The moment Two Stones appeared through the trees, her husband over his shoulder, she'd nearly lost control of her tears. So much relief. And so much fear that he'd been shot.

"Did Sampson say anything? Did he hear their plans while he was in the camp?" Miles spoke up for the first time.

She shook her head. "He's not been conscious since I've seen him." A thought slipped in. "Except... he said a few words. Almost like fever delirium. I think he said my father's name. And McPharland's." She thought back through those long, dark hours. "I think he said *mine*, but I'm not sure. He was hard to understand."

Eric turned to the other men. "Ready then?"

They all started for the door, even Clara's Uncle Hiram. Clara and Angela met them there to say farewell. Naomi must be back in the bed chamber with Dinah, helping care for Sampson. Grace should join them. See if there was anything she could do.

Instead of going to the door to see Gil off, Jess sank into the chair beside Grace and handed her a steaming mug. "This should help warm you. Lillian's finishing up breakfast. I'm sure you're starved."

Grace took a sip but couldn't help glancing at Jess's face to check her expression. Had something happened between her and Gil? Why didn't she go to say goodbye to him?

Maybe Jess overheard her thoughts, for she said, "We'd already talked about what to do if we got news the danger was coming this way. Gil will stay here to help guard the house while Jude, Eric, Miles, and Hiram ride out to help the others. They've had horses ready in the barn and supplies packed."

Ahh. That made sense.

Jess's expression turned a little sheepish, and she looked down at her hands. "Gil's barely left the yard since I came here. He's determined to be ready if my father comes."

She lifted her gaze, and pain glistened in her eyes. "It was really bad, that night we escaped the caves. Gil had been beaten nearly as bad as Sampson, and my father had guards blocking all the exits." Sadness thickened in her expression. "Your father was one of the guards. He stood watch right outside our room. We tried to sneak out through the grass, but he saw us. Somehow, God brought Jude, Miles, and Two Stones at just the right time to whisk us to safety." She let out a long breath, as though still releasing the fear from that night. "It's a wonder, how we got away. And I think Gil's been waiting every minute for the counterattack. He's determined to protect me no matter what."

Her expression softened into the start of a smile, but the sadness lingered. "It's hard, knowing your own father is the one putting the people you love in danger."

The pain deep inside her edged outward, like cracks in ice, spreading from her center. Jess hadn't meant Grace's own father, but she might as well have. The man whose attention and love she'd craved most of her life was now attacking the people who'd taken her in. Who protected her and Ruby. The people she was coming so quickly to love. Especially Sampson.

Before she could respond, the door closed behind Eric, Jude, Hiram, and Miles, settling the room in relative quiet.

Gil sank into a chair at the window, rifle in hand and his focus through the glass.

Clara and Angela had already moved to the kitchen to help Lillian, and Sean went into the bed chamber where Dinah and Naomi sat with Sampson.

Patsy stood a little behind Gil, peering through the window. "You let me know when you're ready for me to spell you."

"I will." His voice came low. Did he plan to allow her to stand guard then? He trusted a woman when there was a chance she might have to shoot a person?

Once more, Jess seemed to hear Grace's unspoken questions. She spoke quietly. "Patsy's a crack shot. Angela too. I think Dinah and Naomi are good also. Makes me wish I'd been able to practice."

Grace nodded, but her mind followed the idea of it. She could shoot a rifle, but she'd rarely practiced her aim. A few times, she and Mama had gone hunting for meat, but she'd never been able to bring herself to pull the trigger on a live animal. It was hard enough to skin and clean one already dead.

She much preferred to eat the food Oren had delivered each month, even the times the meat supply had been too small to last more than a few meals.

What Jess spoke of was something much different, though. Did she really mean she wished she could have the chance to take a human life? Even her own father's if it came down to it? Surely not. She probably wasn't thinking the matter through. Just wanted the chance to be helpful.

"Shall I refill your mug?" Jess reached for the cup Grace held.

Grace shook her head. "I need to put my horse away, then I'll go sit with Sampson."

"Miles took your mare to the barn before they left." Gil spoke up from his seat at the window.

The poor horse had been through so much, carrying two people up and down the mountain slopes for so many hours.

She'd been soaked in sweat when they arrived, and Miles probably wouldn't have been able to take the time to give her a rubdown.

Grace pushed herself to her feet, muscles protesting the movement. "I'll go brush her then. She's earned it."

Jess stood as well and took her empty cup. "I'll come with you to help." Her eyes darted to the window where Gil kept watch.

Grace looked his way too. Would he stop them from going outside?

But he only gave a small nod, his gaze never leaving the tree line beyond the yard.

As Grace pulled on her gloves and crossed to the door, Jess followed her to don coat, hat, and gloves. By the time they stepped out into the icy morning air, the sky had lightened to a pale gray. They descended the hill to the barn, their boots crunching in the snow.

Inside, her mare stood in a stall, already unsaddled and unbridled, a blanket over her back. Miles had been thorough, even with little time.

She stepped inside and ran a hand down the horse's damp neck. "You did so well, girl. Thank you."

Jess appeared with brushes and handed one to Grace. For a few minutes, they worked in silence, the rhythmic swish of the bristles the only sound.

"What else did Sampson say?" Jess finally asked, not looking up from her work on the mare's withers. "You mentioned my father's name."

Grace shook her head, the motion sending a dull ache through her temples. Her exhaustion was returning in force. "Just our fathers' names and the word *mine*. Even those were hard to make out. He was barely conscious most of the way here."

She closed her eyes, remembering the feel of Sampson's

weight against her, the way his head had lolled against her shoulder. She'd been so afraid she'd lose him. That she'd never again see the warmth in his eyes or the curve of his smile.

She swallowed hard against the memories and focused on brushing the mare's flank. She couldn't let herself think the worst. Sampson was strong. He would pull through this. He had to.

Jess's soft voice interrupted her spiraling thoughts. "How are you holding up through all this? It can't be easy, your husband being hurt so badly, and by your own father's men..."

Grace paused in her brushing and met the other woman's empathetic gaze. She tried to muster a smile, but it felt weak. "It's been...hard. I hate that I've brought all this trouble down on Sampson and all of you. If I had never left my cabin, never went to Missoula Mills, never met Sampson..."

"Don't do that." Jess shook her head firmly. "None of this is your fault. Our fathers..." Pain flashed in her eyes. "...they're not good men. They would have come after the Coulters sooner or later, whether you were here or not. Please don't blame yourself."

Tears pricked at Grace's eyes, and she blinked them away. Jess was right, logically she knew that. But the guilt still gnawed at her insides like a persistent rodent. If only she had stayed hidden away from the world, maybe Sampson would be safe and whole right now.

As if reading her mind, Jess reached across the horse's back and rested her hand on Grace's, her voice gentle but insistent. "Sampson doesn't regret a thing."

Grace looked up sharply, searching Jess's face. How could he not wish he'd never laid eyes on her? He was unconscious, badly wounded, because of her choice to leave that lonely valley.

Jess smiled softly. "I don't know him well, but I did talk to him a bit when he was working in my father's mine. And I saw the way he looked at you yesterday morning, when you helped him to the chair after he remembered about Jedidiah's camp." Her smile deepened. "The moment you touched him, his whole demeanor changed. Like you were his anchor in the storm. That kind of bond, that devotion in a man's eyes...it doesn't happen by accident or obligation. Sampson cares for you, Grace. Deeply. I'd stake my life on it."

Grace's heart clenched, painful and wonderful all at once. She wanted to believe Jess's words, wanted it so badly she ached with it.

"I remember the first time I saw that look in Gil's eyes." Jess's gaze turned distant. "We were in the house inside my father's cave and I was cooking breakfast. Gil came over and offered to help. The way he looked at me as he stood there by the cookstove, I nearly melted into a puddle right there on the floor." A wistful smile curved her lips. "Like I was the only woman in the world, and he'd move heaven and earth just to be near me."

Jess's eyes focused back on Grace. "When a Coulter man looks at you that way, you can be sure he's given you his whole heart. Don't doubt it for a second."

Could Sampson really feel that way about her? After all the trouble and heartache knowing her had brought him? It seemed too wonderful to be true. Too much to let herself hope for.

It was dangerous to dream of such things. Hadn't life taught her not to expect affection from a man?

The creak of the barn door made them both jump.

"That's probably Clara coming to hurry us in for breakfast." Jess moved to the stall opening to look out.

But when she poked her head out, her face went bone white. Her eyes were huge as she whispered a single word.

"Papa."

CHAPTER 20

*G*race's pulse pounded in her ears. She peered through the slats of the wooden stall. Jess's father had come? She'd never met Mick McPharland, but the stories were enough to raise her guard.

With the light flooding the opening, she couldn't make out details. But then the barn door creaked shut, and the newcomer came clear.

He wasn't alone.

Her father stood beside the man who must be McPharland.

Her father surveyed the barn's interior with hard eyes, his jaw clenched tight. Searching for her? Or for the Coulters he'd come to destroy?

Her pulse ratcheted higher. How had they gotten past the Coulters? Where were the rest of the men?

The sound of gunfire had become so common that she'd hardly noticed it. Now, it still crackled, but it was closer. Not dangerously so, though. These two must have ridden ahead somehow, slipped through the defenses.

And Gil. Had he seen them enter the barn?

And why had they come? To take her and Jess back with them?

Fresh fear churned in her gut, but she forced it down. She wouldn't go with her father. Not ever. But maybe she could reason with him, persuade him to abandon this terrible plot.

McPharland took a step toward them. "Jessamine." His voice sounded almost tender.

Jess lifted her chin. "What are you doing here?" Unlike her father, anger vibrated on her words.

He spread his hands. "I've come for you. To take you home where you belong."

"I'm not going anywhere with you. Take your men and leave."

McPharland stepped closer, and as he did, his gaze caught on Grace through the cracks in the stall wall. His eyes narrowed. "Who's this?"

Her father strode to McPharland's side. "Grace? What in blazes are you doing here?"

Fury surged through her, infusing her with the courage to step out from her hiding place and face her father head-on. "I came for Sampson, to help him after what your men did to him." She lifted her chin. "And I came to stop you from hurting anyone else."

Father's eyes turned to flint, cold and unyielding. "This has nothing to do with you."

"It has everything to do with me. These people took me in, showed me kindness. I won't let you destroy them." Anger pulsed through her.

"Kindness?" he scoffed. "They turned you against your own flesh and blood."

"No." Grace shook her head. "You did that all on your own." She grasped for one more thread of courage. "If you care about me at all, you'll leave here. Leave the Coulters alone."

His face remained hard, his jaw clenched tight, his eyes

glinting like cold steel in the dim light filtering through the barn slats. "I've put my whole focus on getting what we want from the Coulters. That's more important than anything else. More important than you."

His words pierced like a knife, severing her heart. She could only stare at him. Where was the father she once knew? Or thought she had known. His expression held nothing soft. No warmth, no compassion, no love. Only an icy, unwavering resolve.

"And if you can't abide that," he continued in that same icy tone, "then you're no daughter of mine."

The words slammed into her like a physical blow, driving the air from her lungs. She staggered back a step, eyes blurring.

Jess gripped her arm, holding her steady.

Grace blinked to clear her eyes, forcing herself to straighten. She couldn't let him see how much he'd hurt her. Couldn't give him the satisfaction.

Beside her, Jess straightened, and a glance at her profile showed her jaw set. "Both of you need to leave. Now." Her voice rang out strong and clear in the tense stillness of the barn. "Or I'll call the entire Coulter clan, and they'll be more than happy to force you off their land."

Her father let out a harsh bark of laughter, the sound grating against Grace's ears. "I'd like to see you try, girl." He took a menacing step toward Jess, his weathered face twisting into a sneer. "In fact, it would be mighty helpful to have them all gathered together. Make things simpler."

Icy tendrils of fear snaked through Grace's veins as the weight of his words sank in.

How could she have ever thought her father cared enough to listen to her pleas? That there was anything left inside him besides callous self-interest and hate? Nausea roiled in her stomach.

She darted a glance at the barn door. The only other exit was a stall farther down that opened to the corral. But their fathers blocked them from leaving this stall. She and Jess would have to get past them to escape.

She darted a glance at the rifle Jess had left propped in the corner of the stall. It was close, so close. If she could just get her hands on it...

But even as the thought crossed her mind, doubt followed swift on its heels. Could she really do it? Point a gun at her own father and pull the trigger? At anyone?

She had to try. For Jess. For Sampson and his entire family.

In a lightning-quick move, she snatched up the rifle and brought it to her shoulder, sighting down the barrel at her father's chest. Her hands shook, but she gripped the stock tight, finger poised over the trigger.

The man she'd always thought of as Father stared at her for a long moment, then a slow grin spread over his face, and he laughed. Actually *laughed*.

The sound came harsh and mocking. "What in the world do you think you're doing, girl? Put that toy down before you hurt yourself." Then any hint of humor leaked from his expression, leaving only cold fury. "Who do you think you are to point a gun at me?"

Anger surged through Grace, hot and bright. She had no trouble holding the rifle steady now. "I am Grace Hampton Coulter." As the words left her mouth, she absorbed the truth of them, soaking them into every part of her. "And this is my home, my family."

She met his gaze without flinching, letting him see the resolve in her eyes. "I will not let you hurt them anymore. I won't let you destroy the only good thing—"

Her father's hand shot out, knocking the rifle sideways.

She stumbled, her grip faltering as the weapon slipped from her grip. Before she could recover, her father lunged forward, his fingers digging into her arms like iron bands.

Panic exploded through her as he dragged her out of the stall, his strength overpowering. She thrashed against him, desperate to break free, but he held her fast. He wrapped an arm around her, clamping her tight against him, holding her wrists with his other hand. His foul breath blew hot against her ear.

"You've made your choice." His growl coiled more fear inside her. "Now you'll pay the price."

From the corner of her eye, she could just see McPharland snatch up the fallen rifle, leveling it between her and Jess. She couldn't see his expression, but she didn't have to. He was just like her father. Heartless.

Her captor—she couldn't bring herself to think of him as Father anymore—clamped the arm around her tighter as he let her wrists go to reach for a coil of rope hanging on a nearby post. Her pulse surged into a panicked gallop as he wound the rough fibers around her upper body, pinning her arms to her sides.

The rope bit into her flesh, the pain secondary to the utter helplessness that washed over her. How had it come to this? How had she let herself believe that she could stand against him, that she could protect those she loved?

Tears burned behind her eyes, and she could no longer hold them back.

Jess stood frozen, her face pale and stricken. Grace wanted to call out to her, to tell her to run, to save herself, but the words lodged in her throat, choking her.

McPharland's voice cut through the tense silence. "What are you doing, Jedidiah?"

Her father jerked the knot tight, pulling her off balance with the action. "I'm doing what needs to be done. They made their bed. They betrayed us. Now they get to lie in it."

McPharland's voice lost a bit of its fury. "She's your daughter. Your flesh and blood."

Jedidiah's laughter was bitter, mocking. "You've gone soft,

Mick, letting sentiment cloud your judgment. There's no other way. This ends here, today. One way or another. No loose ends."

She could barely breathe through her panic. Especially with the rope cinched so tightly around her chest.

Her own father was about to kill her. And Jess too.

God, help us! Nothing but a miracle could save them. They were at the mercy of a man who possessed none. God had kept Sampson alive. Maybe He would choose to protect her and Jess too.

Her father jerked her backward, and she scrambled to find footing as he half-dragged her to another stall. Then he shoved her hard, sending her sprawling onto dirty straw. When she hit the ground, pain lanced through her shoulder.

She struggled to sit up, to see what was happening outside the stall. What would they do to Jess?

The rope was cinched too tight, and she couldn't get her balance. Frustrated tears blurred her vision as she strained, desperate for some glimpse of Jess, to know what was being done to her.

Outside the stall, she could only hear silence, broken by the distant sound of gunfire and the ragged gasps of her own breathing.

Until McPharland's voice cut through the stillness like a knife. "Don't touch my daughter." The words came low, danger-ous, filled with a cold fury that sent shivers down her spine.

"Fine, if you want her to come with us, she can." Her father sounded hesitant now.

A flicker of hope sparked to life in her chest. Maybe there was still a chance for Jess, a way out of this nightmare. She finally pushed herself up on her knees and peered through the cracks in the stall door.

McPharland stood with the rifle pointed at her father, his face a mask of cold fury. "The thing is..." His voice came low and dangerous. "...I'm not sure I want you coming. I knew you were ruthless, but a man who would take his own daughter's life? That's not someone I can have around."

Jedidiah's eyes flashed with disbelief. "What are you saying, Mick? We're in this together. Always have been."

McPharland shook his head, the rifle's aim never wavering. "Not anymore. I can't let you do this, Jed."

Grace's pulse pounded. She hardly dared to breathe. Was this really happening? Was Jess's father actually standing up to hers?

Father's expression shifted from surprise to calculation. "You're making a mistake, Mick." His voice had turned deceptively calm. "We're so close to getting everything we've worked for. Don't throw it away over some misguided sentiment."

McPharland's jaw clenched. "It's not sentiment. It's about having a line you don't cross. Hurting your own child…that's too far, even for the likes of us." His tone was hard as flint. "Sorry it has to end this way, but I have to protect my daughter. And yours too, even if you won't."

The gun exploded.

The deafening blast thundered as powder clouded around him. For a moment, everything seemed to still, the world holding its breath in the aftermath of the shot.

Then her father crumpled to the ground, his body hitting the earth with a dull thud.

CHAPTER 21

A scream caught in Grace's throat as she stared at her father's prone form. Blood seeped from his chest, staining his coat in a wide crimson circle. She couldn't breathe, couldn't think. Couldn't move.

Dimly, she heard McPharland speaking, his voice low and urgent as he addressed Jess. "I won't make you come with me. You can stay with Coulter if that's what you really want. But you can come home anytime." He paused, gaze flicking to the barn door. "I have to leave before that shot brings people. I'll take my men back, and I won't bother the Coulters again. I give you my word."

Jess murmured something Grace couldn't understand, and Grace forced herself to blink. To come out of this stupor so she could do something. Say something.

She barely caught the flash of Jess's father as he sprinted past her. He slipped into the stall that led to the corral. And then he was gone.

Jess appeared in front of her, hands resting on Grace's shoulders. "Are you hurt?"

Grace forced herself to focus on the question, then shook

her head. Not outwardly. Inside, she couldn't tell how bad things were. Could a person be numb and in agony at the same time? Cold had settled in her bones.

Gil would be here soon, surely. He must have been distracted when her father and McPharland slipped into the barn, but he couldn't have missed the gunshot.

"Can you stand so I can untie you?"

Grace nodded and let Jess help her to her feet. Then Jess leaned down to focus on the knot in the rope around Grace. The rope her *father* had bound her with.

Jedidiah. Not her father. No true father would treat his child like that.

Jess's fingers trembled as she worked, her breath uneven.

Grace could feel the other woman's panic, a mirror of her own, as they both tried to avoid looking at Jedidiah's lifeless body.

The barn door pushed open, and Grace's heart leaped into her throat. Had McPharland come back around the front? Surely not. That must be Gil, coming because of the gunshot.

As a figure peered inside, she strained to make out the features.

Her heart knew the difference even before her mind realized it.

Sampson.

A half-cry, half-sob surged from her chest.

The door pushed wider as he stepped in—nay, charged in. Another figure came behind him. Dinah.

"What happened?" Sampson ran to her, his gaze taking them in. When his focus snagged on her father, he nearly stumbled to a stop, but then his eyes moved back to her. His look was so intense, just like the man she'd known before her father had had him nearly killed.

"My father and Jedidiah were here." Jess stepped back from her focus on the knot to face the newcomers. "Jedidiah was going to kill us, but my father...he stood up for us. He shot Jedidiah."

Emotions surged across Sampson's face as he comprehended Jess's words. Shock. Anger. And then something Grace had never seen on him—on any man. He focused on her with a look that held so much...possessiveness. His eyes sharpened into something almost feral.

He closed the final stride between them and wrapped his good arm around her, pulling her tight against him. With his broken arm still wrapped, he couldn't fully envelop her, but she nestled into his warmth anyway. His scent, his strength, the steady drum of his heartbeat against her cheek—it all said *home* in a way she'd never known before.

Just minutes before, she'd thought she would never see him again, never feel his embrace. Her hands were still bound, preventing her from returning the hug, but she pressed as close as she could.

"Are you hurt?" Sampson's voice was low and urgent in her ear.

"No." Not physically at least. Her heart...well, she'd have to deal with that later.

The barn door swung open again and she tensed, but it was Gil rushing in, his expression wild. "I heard a shot. What—" He froze, taking in the scene before him.

"We're all right," Jess called out to him, and Gil surged toward her. She met him partway and he wrapped her in his arms.

Jess murmured something to him, probably telling what happened. Gil pulled back to look at her face, his expression transforming the same way Sampson's had. From relief to simmering anger. He pulled away from Jess and ran toward them, pulling out his knife and handing it to Dinah.

"I have to go after McPharland." Gil started toward the stall that opened to the corral.

"Gil, wait!" Jess sprinted after him.

Gil paused and turned to her, and Jess grabbed his arm.

"Please. My father promised he would leave us alone. Can we just...let it be over?" Her blue eyes shimmered with tears.

For a long moment, Gil stared down at her, clearly torn. Then finally he nodded. "If you're sure that's what you want."

Jess nodded, her whole body sagging with relief as Gil pulled her into his arms again.

He held her close, his body surrounding her as if he could shield her from the world. "I'm so sorry I wasn't here. I saw a man at the edge of the woods, but then he was gone. He must have been a distraction, so I didn't see them come in. I didn't know anyone was here until I heard the shot."

Dinah managed to slice through the ropes binding Grace's hands, and as soon as she was free, Grace turned fully into Sampson's embrace, wrapping her arms around his waist and burying her face in his chest. She didn't squeeze in case it hurt his ribs, just relished the contact. The feel of him settled the last of the tremors still running through her body.

Sampson's face pressed into the hair at her neck, his good hand sliding up and down her back as he held her tight against him. Neither of them spoke. Maybe he needed to feel her as much as she did him.

Dinah had moved to crouch beside her father's body. She would know what to check. A moment later, she stood and moved to Grace's side, rubbing a gentle hand across her shoulders.

Grace adjusted her head against Sampson's chest so she could see Dinah's expression. The sadness in her eyes said everything.

"I'm so sorry, Grace."

Grace wouldn't have thought the words would bring such a rush of tears, but she did her best to hold them back as she nodded. If she spoke, she'd lose control completely.

Dinah gave a final rub across her shoulders, then stepped back. "We should head up to the house. Probably the both of you should be in bed." She gave a pointed look between Sampson and Grace.

Grace forced herself to straighten and pull back a little so she could see Sampson's face. "How did you make it all the way down here?" She could see the pain lines around his eyes, but he looked so much better than when his brothers had carried him into the house. "You weren't conscious the last time I saw you."

One corner of his mouth tugged a little. "Dinah can work wonders." He slid a look at his sister-in-law.

Dinah's snort told Grace what she thought of that. But then she stepped closer and rested a hand on Sampson's good shoulder as she spoke to Grace. "This, my dear, is a combination of laudanum, a good stiff bandage, and a very stubborn husband who had to lay eyes on his wife as soon as he was coherent enough to realize she wasn't at his side."

Sampson's hold on Grace tightened, telling her that Dinah's teasing wasn't far off the mark. He spoke lower. "I couldn't shake the feeling something was wrong. I just needed to see you."

She snuggled in closer, letting herself relish this feeling of safety. Of having someone who would push through pain and anything else to protect her. Or even just to see her.

"All right, everyone. To the house. Now." Dinah's voice took on a no-nonsense tone.

Grace let Sampson and Dinah guide her out of the barn, Jess and Gil following. The short walk to the house felt surreal, her mind still struggling to process all that had happened. Her father was gone. Truly gone this time. And the man beside her— the man she'd been forced to marry—had become her anchor in the storm.

As they approached, the front door opened and the rest of the family spilled out onto the snow, their faces etched with worry. Naomi held Ruby, bundled in a cocoon of blankets and drinking from her feeding bottle. Safe and content.

"What happened?" Sean demanded as he ran toward them.

Gil relayed the events in the barn, and the others listened in stunned silence.

"How awful." Patsy broke the quiet first, and it seemed to release a dam of questions and exclamations from the others.

Sampson still had his arm around Grace, as hers were around him. Was he swaying? She glanced up at him, taking in the beads of sweat on his brow and the tight lines of pain around his mouth. He was pushing himself too hard.

She leaned closer to his ear. "You should go back to bed. We're all safe now and you need to rest."

He shook his head. "I'm not leaving you."

Tears pricked her eyes at his words, at the fierce protectiveness in his gaze. She had never had someone put her first, not like this.

Swallowing down the lump in her throat, she tightened her grip around his waist. "Then I'll stay with you."

His gaze softened and he nodded, letting her guide him past the crowd.

They made their way slowly up the two steps into the cabin, and Sampson breathed heavier by the time they maneuvered through the main room. Once in the bed chamber, he eased down onto the mattress.

"Do you want to take off your boots?" With the other men still out fighting, he might want to keep fully dressed so he could be ready at a moment's notice.

But he shouldn't be going anywhere. And with McPharland calling off his attack, hopefully the rest of the Coulters and braves would return soon.

Sampson nodded and reached with his good hand to pull off the first shoe.

She crouched to take care of it for him.

"You don't have to do that." He gave a half-hearted protest. But he probably knew as well as she did that he needed help.

"I want to." She kept her focus on tugging off the first boot, then placing it neatly by the bedpost. This felt like such a wifely duty, helping her husband to bed, removing his clothing. Heat flamed up her neck. Not his clothing, just his boots.

When she finished, Sampson let out a relieved sigh. "Thank you."

She stood and fluffed his pillow as he eased back. His face twisted in a grimace, and he hissed out a breath as his body sank into the mattress. His eyelids lowered to half-mast, and his breathing lightened, like he was focusing on tiny inhales.

"Are your ribs hurting a great deal?" She pulled the quilts up over his legs.

"A little." So *yes*.

She settled the blankets at his middle, then stepped back to look over him. "Would you like a drink of water?"

He opened his eyes, taking her in. Then he lifted the side of the blanket to reveal the empty mattress on his good side. "Will you...stay with me?"

She glanced at the bed. He didn't mean sit. He meant...lie with him. Everything in her wanted to fill that empty place, to snuggle into his side and let him hold her. To soak in his comfort. His strength. To be there for anything he might need.

They both wore clothes, and he was too hurt to do much but breathe. And they *were* married, after all. It felt like much should be said before—or rather *if*—they ever became married in the full sense of the word, but she wouldn't deny him her presence.

For now, she would simply lie beside him.

Sampson must have thought her silence meant refusal, for he started to let the blanket fall back into place.

She stepped closer and took the cover from him. She needed to slip her own boots off first, a process which she fumbled her way through. Her pulse had picked up its pace again. Maybe she should just pull up a chair to sit beside him.

But her shoes were off now. She had to be careful not to lie where she would put pressure on his injuries. She sat and pulled her feet up onto the bed. This mattress was far too narrow for two grown people, especially when one of them possessed the broad shoulders of Sampson Coulter.

He held out his arm though. "Put your head on my shoulder."

She obeyed, lying on her side with her temple resting on the solid bulk of his shoulder. He wrapped his arm around her, settling his hand on the small of her waist. Cradling her in his strength.

She let her body relax, one breath at a time. She didn't have enough room to put both her hands between them, so she moved one to rest on his chest. Up high, where hopefully it wouldn't hurt his ribs.

Her pulse thrummed through her ears. But the longer she rested there, the more her body settled.

Sampson's thumb stroked up and down the back of her arm. A slow steady rhythm that soothed her insides little by little.

But though her body relaxed, her mind refused to follow.

Images of her father flashed through her thoughts. That cold hatred in his eyes when he'd said she was no daughter of his. The rough way he'd gripped her wrists when he'd jerked her out of the stall. The raw burn of the rope as he tied her. Each image pulled the tears closer to the surface. Each memory ripped a new gash in her heart.

One tear slid free, scalding a path down her cheek to land on Sampson's shirt. Then another. A ragged breath shuddered out of her chest. The tears she'd been holding back finally spilled over.

Her father was dead.

The man who was supposed to love and protect her had tried to kill her.

And now, he was gone forever.

Sampson's arm tightened around her, pulling her closer. He tucked her head under his chin. "I'm so sorry, Grace." His deep voice rumbled through his chest. "I'm here. I've got you."

She couldn't speak past the emotion in her throat, so she just nodded against him. Her fingers curled into his shirt, and quiet sobs shook her frame.

CHAPTER 22

*S*ampson stood at the edge of the clearing, his good arm wrapped around Grace's slender waist as they gazed at the six freshly turned graves. The tiny mounds of earth seemed so small, so insignificant to mark the loss of a life.

Beside them, Dinah cradled baby Ruby close to her chest, her eyes red-rimmed. Around them, the rest of their family waited in reverent silence.

Sampson swallowed hard against the knot in his throat. Three days since the shootout that had taken Jedidiah and five of his men. Three days that felt like an eternity.

McPharland and his men had faded away, as Jess said he'd promised to do. Some of Two Stones braves found the stash of blasting powder—still useable, though that seemed hard to believe after so much travel and time in the snow.

For now, they'd decided to store it far enough away from the house that an accidental explosion couldn't do damage. Maybe they'd stake a claim on the neighboring land where Two Stones had found the sapphires and start a new mine. It was far enough away that it would be hard to work from the main house.

Maybe he and Grace could build a home there. He'd become

even better at mining after spending so many months heaving a pickax in McPharland's caves.

But that could be a decision for later.

He glanced at Grace. Loose strands of her hair lifted in the light breeze. Her eyes, those captivating blue depths that had first drawn him in, were rimmed with red, evidence of the countless tears she'd spilled since that horrible moment. Yet even in her sorrow, there was a strength about her, a quiet resilience that made his chest clench.

The past three days had been a whirlwind of emotion. He and Grace had spent much of the time tucked away in their chamber. She'd talked...really talked. Telling stories from her years of growing up with only her mother in the little house in the valley. About her father's visits each month, and the way his final actions tainted everything that had come before.

Sampson held her every time she wept, her slender frame shaking with the force of her sobs as she'd mourned the loss of the father she'd never truly had. The realization that Jedidiah's love had been a façade, that he'd turned against her in the end, no show of regret or wavering commitment, had shattered something deep within her.

She'd even shared everything she knew about Ruby's parents. About the quiet man who'd delivered supplies each month to her and her mother. About the mail-order bride he'd sent for, who was widowed and with child. How the last time he came with a delivery, he'd said his new wife died in childbirth, and he was at his wit's end with caring for the babe who'd survived. A few women from the saloon were trying to help him, but he wasn't sure how long he could manage. That had been the last time she saw the man before Ruby showed up on her doorstep.

Sampson could imagine the desperation of a man who suddenly found himself caring for a newborn, especially a babe as tiny and fragile as Ruby. And one look at Grace could easily convince a fellow she would be a loving and capable mother. Yet after holding Ruby even once, the thought of giving her up... He couldn't imagine the turmoil that poor man must have struggled through.

But that decision had brought Ruby into Grace's life, and now Sampson's. And he could only be thankful.

Grace had asked about Sampson's life, too, and she seemed to love all the stories of adventures and mishaps with his brothers and Two Stones. And Lucy, the sister who'd been gone so long now.

Jude's voice broke the group's stillness. "It's hard to know what to say about deaths like these. God loved them, from the very beginning. And He never stopped loving them, trying to reach them, even to the end. Yet He gives us free choice to accept His love or push it away."

Beneath his arm, Grace took in a shaky breath.

They'd talked about God these past few days, and what accepting His love could look like. She'd never known truly unconditional love—as much as it sounded like her mother had loved her, a few details Grace shared made him think her mother might have lived in fear, or perhaps a lingering melancholy.

Sampson couldn't blame the woman, given the lonely life she'd been forced to live, to raise her only child alone. But Grace had never seen a model of the kind of love God offered.

God, help me be an example for her. Help me love her the way You love us. Unconditionally.

Jericho cleared his throat. "Lord, we ask for Your comfort and peace in this time of loss. May the darkest moments draw us closer to You. May we feel Your love in all its fullness."

Lillian began to sing, her clear soprano voice lifting the familiar words of "Amazing Grace" into the crisp winter air. The others joined in, their voices blending in the hymn.

Grace must not know the song, for she didn't sing. But she

leaned her head on his shoulder, her body warm and soft against his side. He tightened his arm around her.

This woman had burrowed so deep into his heart that he couldn't imagine a life without her. When her grief eased some, he would ask to court her properly. He would work every day to show her the depth of his love and commitment.

Then, Lord willing, they would build a future together—here on the ranch, at the new claim, or wherever her heart desired. He would spend his days cherishing her and Ruby.

As the final notes of the hymn faded into the stillness, Grace turned to him. Her eyes glistened with tears, but they held a light too. A small smile even curved her lips.

Then she stepped away from him, reaching to take Ruby from Dinah's arms.

"Hi there, sweet girl." Grace held her up so they could see eye to eye, then snuggled her close, nuzzling Ruby's downy head.

The baby gurgled in response, a sound of pure contentment.

His chest ached at the sight. His girls. Grace looked lighter already, as if a layer of sorrow had fallen away.

Thank You, Lord.

Jericho stepped up beside him, resting a hand on his good shoulder. "It's good to see you up, looking more like yourself."

Sampson nodded. "I feel more like myself." He'd taken half the usual dose of laudanum this afternoon, and his ribs only ached if he moved wrong. His arm felt a lot better too. Maybe he could finally quit the stuff fully. It clouded his mind so much, and Grace and their daughter deserved the best of him.

His entire family, for that matter, though they'd continued to prove how much they still loved him, even at his worst.

Jericho squeezed his shoulder. "It's awfully good to have you home."

Sampson reached for strength to meet his gaze. "It's good to be home."

Jericho's eyes held a gentle smile, the edges creasing a little. "It's a new day. A new beginning for all of us."

Sampson nodded, his throat tight. Maybe this was the time he needed to speak to all of his brothers. They all still lingered around the graves, talking in small clusters.

He raised his voice a little. "I need to apologize. To all of you."

The group turned silent once more, all eyes on him.

He forced himself to keep talking. "For trusting the wrong people. For letting all our sapphires get stolen." He met Jude's gaze so he would see the extent of his regret. Jude only watched him, his head tipped almost in curiosity.

Sampson had to keep going, so he shifted his focus to Gil. "For thinking I could fix my mistakes by myself."

"Just glad you came to your senses." Miles broke in, interrupting his speech.

"Yep. You came around, and that's all we care about." This from Jonah, who'd moved beside him. Close enough to reach out and ruffle Sampson's hair.

Sampson ducked away, and a glance at Jonah's face showed a devilish twinkle that reminded him too much of the pranks they used to play as boys. A lighter time that tugged another layer of weight off his chest. Could his brothers really joke about this?

"Next time, just ask for help instead of joining the enemy. All right?" Jude stepped next to him and clamped a hand on his good shoulder. "We're here. All of us. Anytime. For anything." He gave a squeeze, then let go.

Sampson nodded. "Thanks."

A fresh start. Just like Jericho said.

Maybe he wasn't worthy of his family's love, but they were proving they loved him anyway. Unconditionally. Just as he was learning to love Grace.

As if sensing his thoughts, Grace glanced up, meeting his

gaze over the top of Ruby's head. Her eyes sparkled with a tentative hope, a glimmer of the joy opening up inside him too.

A new beginning for them both.

~

*G*race blinked awake as shafts of pale winter sunlight slanted through the window behind them. A new morning.

She glanced at Sampson to make sure she hadn't awakened him with her movements. The laudanum usually had a firm hold on him in the mornings, and it took a while for him to come out of sleep.

His rich brown eyes stared back at her, less than a foot away.

Heat crept up to her cheeks at his direct look, but she allowed herself to smile. "Good morning." Waking up in Sampson's bed—in Sampson's arms—had become her favorite part of each day.

They both slept fully clothed, of course. But she felt so...safe here.

That first time she'd laid in his arms and cried, something about his presence brought comfort, and he'd continued to bring comfort every time she needed it. The first night, he'd invited her to sleep there. The bed was so small that she had to lie with her head on his shoulder, snuggled into his side. He always kept his good arm around her, his hand resting on the curve of her waist. She'd never felt so warm and cherished. And safe.

He still watched her now, those warm eyes taking her in. "Morning." His voice held that deep sleep-roughness, making a tingle slip through her. The man had no right to be so handsome, with those strong features and heart-stopping eyes. His gaze held a clarity this morning that hadn't been there since his injuries.

"What are you doing?" She tried not to look as shy as she felt.

His gaze roamed her face. "You're so beautiful." He met her eyes again. "If I could, I would lie here and look at you all the time. Never sleep."

Heat surged to her cheeks, probably turning her ears red. But his words wrapped around her heart, filling her with so much warmth. They'd talked a great deal these past few days, but they hadn't broached the subject of their marriage or what the future might hold.

She'd caught an appreciative gaze every now and then, but he'd not spoken to her like this, with such open admiration.

And she had no idea how to respond.

The last thing she wanted was to say the wrong thing and stop whatever he might say or do next. She craved him to be her husband in every sense of the word. A true partner, not just the arrangement he'd initially proposed when her father forced their hasty wedding.

Sampson's mouth curved in a rueful smile. "The hardest part of this broken arm is not being able to touch you the way I want to. To run my finger down your cheek and feel if it's really as soft as it looks." His eyes traced the path he described.

She felt the caress all the way to her toes.

His eyes moved back to hers, and the longing there stole her breath. "I want to kiss you, Grace." His voice rumbled through her. "But...I won't unless you want me to."

Every fiber of her being ached for his kiss, but the words stuck in her throat. He was being so bold, laying his feelings bare. She had to work up the courage to do the same.

Slowly, she reached out and placed her hand on his cheek, something she'd never dared to do before. He'd shaved the day before, and stubble pricked her palm.

Her thumb wandered to his mouth, tracing the contour of his lower lip. Sampson turned enough to place a kiss on the pad of her thumb.

The gesture drew her gaze back up to his eyes. Their brown had turned nearly black with a desire that made her insides quiver.

Yet still he held himself back, not pushing for more than she was ready to give. This man, her husband, was attuned to her in a way no one else had ever been.

That fact gave her the courage to say the words. "I want you to kiss me."

The heat stayed dark in his gaze, even as his eyes somehow turned soft. He shifted, rising up on his good elbow to hover over her. Slowly, reverently, he lowered his mouth to hers.

The first brush of his lips sent a shiver through her. So tender, yet so exquisitely intense. He pulled back the slightest bit, his breath mingling with hers, before capturing her mouth again.

And again.

Every caress of his lips cherished her in a way she had never imagined possible. His kisses journeyed from her lips to her chin, then along her jawline.

When his mouth neared her ear, Sampson murmured in that deep, velvety voice that sent fresh heat coursing through her veins. "You are everything I never knew I needed."

The aching sincerity in those words undid her. She gripped his shirt with one hand and slid the other up his neck and into his hair.

He returned to her mouth with a low growl, the kiss deepening, intensifying. She could feel the barely restrained power thrumming through him, yet he remained gentle. Not pushing her farther than she was ready to go.

At last he pulled back, his breathing heaving as hard as hers. He dropped his forehead to her shoulder as he sucked in air, his shoulders rising with each inhale. Somehow, this felt every bit as intimate as the kiss.

She grazed her fingers over his scalp, relishing the softness of his hair.

He let out another groan, then lifted his head to gaze into her eyes once more. A flicker of uncertainty touched their depths. Did he want her to say something?

Her mind still reeled from the intensity of that kiss. She could barely form coherent thoughts, let alone put them into words. She longed for Sampson to kiss her again, to lose herself in him.

But a small, cautious voice whispered that she wasn't quite ready for where that might lead. Everything about this was so new.

His eyes searched hers, as if seeking assurance he hadn't overstepped. "Grace." His voice was low, rough with emotion. "Can I...would you allow me to court you?"

Relief washed through her, loosening the tightness in her chest. Maybe he realized how new this was for her. And this man, her husband, was making her feel safe and treasured, just like he did in every other way.

She nodded, a soft smile curving her lips. "I would like that very much."

His answering grin sent another flutter through her middle. He turned his head to press a kiss to the skin on the inside of her wrist.

Then he pulled back, enough to sit upright. "I guess it's time I get up."

She reached for his arm, halting him. She needed to give voice to the feelings welling up inside her, the emotions she'd been grappling with these past days as they'd spent so much time together.

He looked at her expectantly, his expression open and encouraging. She took a steadying breath. "Sampson. I just want you to know how thankful I am that you're my husband. Truly."

He stilled, his eyes taking on a sheen. He didn't speak for a long moment, just studied her face as if memorizing every detail. Then he leaned close again to brush the gentlest of kisses across her lips, a bare whisper of contact that somehow conveyed the depth of his feelings more than any words could.

When he pulled back, his gaze locked with hers. The emotion there made her chest ache.

"I'm the one who's thankful, Grace. More than you can possibly know." His voice was low, thick with feeling. "I've been thanking God every day, for bringing you into my life. Even when I was being stubborn and selfish, staying out in the bunkhouse, deep down I knew you were the best thing that ever happened to me."

He reached out to brush a strand of hair from her face, his fingers lingering on her cheek. "You are God's grace to me, you and Ruby both. A better gift than I could have dreamed of. I'll never stop being thankful for you."

Tears pricked her eyes at the raw honesty in his words. This was what she had longed for her entire life, without even realizing it.

A home. A place to belong. Someone to cherish her, body and soul.

CHAPTER 23

*T*he scent of pine needles and cinnamon mingled with woodsmoke from the hearth fire as Sampson settled on the floor, his back pressed against the log wall. His wounded arm rested in a sling across his chest now, instead of in the tight binding Dinah had made him wear the first few days.

Grace eased down beside him, tucking herself under his good arm as she adjusted Ruby in her lap.

Grace spoke to the newborn. "Do you want to see what's happening?" She turned the babe outward, propping the child against her so she could watch the festive scene all around them.

After being away from his family for so long, then nearly losing his life a week ago at the hands of Jedidiah's men, the simple joy of being surrounded by loved ones was a precious gift.

And now, with the danger passed, they could finally all enjoy a proper Christmas. And what a celebration it was turning out to be.

The entire family had gathered, filling the cabin with chatter and laughter. His brothers had brought in a large fir tree that stood in the corner, adorned with garland, ribbons, and a few ornaments their mother and Lucy had made.

The meal had been a great big affair, with roasted venison, turkey, potatoes, fresh bread, and so many sweets he might not eat for days. Now it was time for the exchange of gifts.

"C'mon, Uncle Jericho." Anna bounced in her chair as she and Sean waited none too patiently for everyone to gather by the fire.

"C'mon. C'mon." Little Mary Ellen jumped up and down as she chanted. She hadn't yet been confined to a seat.

How could that much enthusiasm not make even the grumpiest face smile?

Ruby gurgled and waved her hands at her cousins' antics. Her palm landed on Sampson's finger, where he had his hand wrapped around Grace. The babe gripped hard.

Warmth curled through him at the feel of her chubby hand clutching his. He would never, ever tire of the honor of being this tiny girl's father. Of getting to experience all her reactions. Her first smiles, her first laugh.

And now, her first Christmas.

Grace lifted her chin to him with a smile. "She's got you wrapped around her little finger." Amusement tinged her soft voice.

Sampson chuckled. "I suppose so. Both of you." He brushed a kiss against Grace's temple, breathing in the sweet scent of her hair.

When everyone finally settled, Lillian was given the honor of distributing the wrapped parcels. As each gift was opened, laughter and exclamations of delight filled the room. Toys for the children, both handmade and ordered from the States. Beautifully embroidered shawls for all the women—including Grace. That must be Naomi's handiwork. She could accomplish miracles with her needle, and in such a short time. The way his family included Grace and Ruby made him more grateful than he could say.

Miles had outdone his usual hand-crafted gifts this year, especially with what he gave Jericho—one of Dat's old broken rifles, fully repaired and restored with an elaborate carving in the stock. That boy had talent, no question about it.

Or rather, that *man*. Miles looked all grown up with Clara at his side. His eyes held a maturity that hadn't been there before Sampson left. A steadiness.

Clara's uncle joined in just like he'd always been part of the family. It was clear he had a soft spot for the youngsters, propping Mary Ellen on his lap to admire her new doll and hair ribbons.

After the last gift had been opened, Jericho stepped toward the middle and cleared his throat.

The chatter quieted as all eyes turned to him.

"I have one more thing." He paused, looking a little sheepish to command so much attention. "This is mostly for my brothers. Well, I guess maybe it's more for everyone."

The chuckle that circulated made Jericho's ears turn red. It'd been a while since Sampson had seen him flustered, even a little.

Jericho cleared his throat again as he pushed on. "We're all grown men now, most of us with families of our own. I've tried to lead and guide you as best I could, but though my intentions were always good—" He slid a glance at Dinah. "I know my determination to keep people off the ranch wasn't always the best choice."

He paused, his gaze scanning the room. Landing on each person who'd found their way here despite Jericho's efforts. "All you ladies who've come to join us make this place better." His expression turned wry. "You sure make my brothers better." Then he slid a glance sideways. "Even you, Eric."

A round of chuckles sounded. Though a hint of nervousness

threaded through it. Was this merely an apology? Or did Jericho have something to announce?

His face turned sober. "With all those men who came to attack the ranch and mine, I don't think this place is still a secret. Thankfully, God's been working on me a couple years now, helping me rest in Him. Trust that He's taking care of all of us, even if it's not the way I'd do it. His way actually turns out much better in the long run." He glanced at Dinah with an intimate smile.

Then he faced the rest of them. "Anyway, I think it's time for a change. What about if we split the ranch land into seven equal parts, one for each sibling? I'll hold Lucy's portion until Lilly and Sean are old enough."

Whoa.

Split up the ranch? The idea felt foreign. Certainly not something he'd ever expect from their protective eldest brother.

The rest of the family seemed as surprised. Murmurs rose as his family spoke to each other, some calling out questions to Jericho.

Jericho's voice rose above the ruckus. "You can each choose which acreage you want, so long as we agree together. I imagine those of you who've already built cabins will want to keep the property around you."

He turned to the couple on the other side of Dinah. "Eric, Naomi. Dinah and I want to share our portion with you."

Eric's brows shot up. "Really? Just the land around our house, right?"

Jericho shook his head. "We'd like to go half and half. This is your home too."

"I...don't know what to say." Eric wove his fingers through Naomi's as grateful tears tracked down her cheeks. "Thank you. Truly."

Before chatter could start up again, Jericho turned to Jude. "We can talk about the fairest way to split up the mine. Maybe you're paid a wage to oversee it, and we split the sapphires, or maybe the rest of us pitch in more and help with that work. We can all decide together how to handle it."

Jude dipped his chin with a nod, but his eyes sparkled.

The group broke out in excited chatter, discussing potential plots and plans for their land.

But Sampson let the news settle fully. He would have his own portion of land, him and Grace. He'd always known he possessed a seventh of the ranch and mine profits, but he'd always thought it'd be a stake in the whole. He'd never imagined Jericho would agree to give them all their very own property, where they could each choose how to manage it. He and Grace could build the home of their dreams.

He stroked his thumb over her side, and she looked up at him. Her gaze shimmered, filled with a happiness that settled his insides with a warm peace. Their own plot of land was just an extra blessing. As long as he had Grace and Ruby, he was home.

But getting to build their life here with all their family—that made the future look even sweeter.

She rested her hand on his knee and smiled up at him. "Merry Christmas, husband."

He couldn't help lowering his mouth to hers for a quick brush—just a taste. "Merry Christmas, Mrs. Coulter."

He had to force himself to lift his head and focus back on the group.

Jericho was watching him, a half-smile curving his mouth. Sampson met his gaze and nodded a quiet thanks.

This would be a new season, a new chapter for the Coulter family.

Jericho stepped back against the wall and wrapped his arm around Dinah's waist with a contented smile.

But Dinah held up her hand. "Hold on, everyone. There's actually one more gift left to open."

Once more, the family fell silent. All eyes turned to her as she faced Jericho with a mischievous glint in her eye. "You should know better than to think you get the final say, my love." From the pocket of her skirt, she produced a small, neatly wrapped package and pressed it into her husband's hands.

Jericho raised an eyebrow, a grin tugging at the corners of his mouth. "Is that so, Doc? And here I thought I was the head of this family."

"Oh, hush and open it." Dinah swatted his arm playfully, her eyes never leaving his face.

As Jericho eased the paper open, anticipation charged the air around them. The wrapping fell away, revealing a piece of folded cloth. Jericho unfolded it, holding up a baby gown.

It's meaning grabbed Sampson at the same instant that Grace gasped.

Realization took a second longer for Jericho, but his eyes widened, and he looked at Dinah, his mouth parted. "Is this...? Are you...?"

Dinah nodded, her smile radiant. "Sometime in the summer, if my calculations are correct."

A heartbeat of silence, and then Jericho let out a whoop of pure joy, sweeping Dinah into his arms and twirling her around.

Laughter erupted from the family, and the room came alive with fresh excitement.

Sampson pulled Grace a little closer, his heart near to bursting with so many wonderful gifts.

Ruby squealed and clapped her hands, as if she too understood the joy rippling through the room.

Grace tilted her head up to him, her own smile soft as her eyes brightened. Again, he pressed a kiss to her mouth. Then he shifted so he could murmur in her ear. "I love you."

One day, maybe he and Grace would share a moment like Jericho and Dinah, announcing a new addition to their own little family. But for now, he already had every blessing he could possibly want.

EPILOGUE 1

*G*race stood with Sampson at her side, little Ruby cradled in his good arm. Most of the Coulter family gathered around them. Waiting for the ceremony.

In the distance, the winter sun glinted off snow-capped peaks. She still hadn't gotten used to the beauty of this place, often catching her breath with fresh wonder.

She never would have guessed this ranch could feel like home so quickly.

She slid a sideways glance at Sampson—her husband. That broad chest, his incredibly handsome face. when he looked at her the way he did now, with such intensity, he made her insides tingle.

And holding Ruby's tiny form, snuggling her so close, so comfortably. *Lord, how could You have blessed me so much?*

Now that Sampson had regained so much strength, he was usually the one holding or carrying the babe. Like he couldn't get enough of her. Like the little pumpkin had him wrapped around her finger.

Which was entirely true.

"I think they're coming." Sean's excited words brought the murmuring of the others to a halt.

They all turned as the cabin's front door opened and Lillian stepped out. The brides must be ready.

Jess and Patsy would both be married today. A shiver of excitement slipped through Grace.

Grace had been inside helping with preparations much of the morning, and both brides had looked angelic. Patsy with her rich auburn curls and Jess with that dark hair and her wide blue eyes. The cabin had been full of so much joy, so much laughter as they'd all bantered and prepared for today's festivities. After the wedding there'd be a feast, and Grace had had a hand in helping to prepare it.

Now, Lillian's sweet face held a shy smile as she descended the single step to the snow-covered ground and moved to the side to hold the door.

A moment later, Jess emerged looking absolutely radiant. The lovely blue gown she wore perfectly accentuated her features, but her smile outshone everything else.

Grace slid a glance at Gil, who waited with Jonah and the deputy who would perform the ceremony. Gil stared at his bride with so much wonder, she almost chuckled. Were his eyes glistening? So much admiration there.

As Jess walked through the open path between the family members, her gaze left Gil for the first time, sliding to look at Grace. Her smile, the warmth in it, felt special.

The two of them had talked a great deal this past week, and she'd learned more about Jess's life in the caves. She was a remarkable woman, strong in ways Grace might never be. Yet so kind and gentle.

All the women on the Coulter ranch could fit that description, and they'd all become friends. Good friends. She'd never had such abundance. Being around so many people wasn't nearly so overwhelming now. The way they included her as if she'd always been part of their family... She never ever wanted to leave this place.

As Jess neared Gil, he stepped forward to close the distance between them, eagerness joining the other emotions in his expression. He took both her hands and lifted them to his mouth. The gentleness, the reverent way he kissed them as he held Jess's gaze... It was a wonder Jess didn't swoon right there in the snow.

Grace might swoon herself. But a glance over at her own husband settled her. He'd been watching the couple with a little smile on his face, but when he met Grace's gaze, the richness of the love in his eyes made her heart swell. This man... *Thank You, Lord. I can never say it enough.*

The way he'd courted her over the past week had felt too wonderful. The gifts he continued to surprise her with, the way he remembered the little things she'd said. And his kisses. They stirred her blood.

But what she'd loved the very most were their long conversations, sometimes sitting by the fire as she fed Ruby, sometimes while he held the sleeping babe. Sometimes, they snuggled in his little bed before they went to sleep each night. She loved his stories, his dreams for the future. She especially loved when he shared his worries or regrets. Everything about this man drew her.

Now that Gil and Jess were settled before the deputy, the group turned back toward the cabin to watch for Patsy. A moment later, Lillian pulled open the door again, and Patsy emerged.

Patsy shone every bit as much as Jess had as she stepped down to the snow and walked toward the group. A sound from behind made Grace glance back. Jonah's grin stretched wide across his face, not holding back a bit of his pleasure.

Patsy approached, her own smile beaming. No shyness, no hesitation. Just pure joy.

At last, both couples stood before Deputy Hansen, the same man who'd married her and Sampson.

She couldn't help another look at her husband. Was he remembering that day the two of them stood in the hotel's parlor for their ceremony? Sampson had brought her a holly branch since there weren't flowers blooming. She should have realized then what a good man he was.

In truth, she *had* known. That was why she'd braved marrying him, even though she'd only met him the day before. His integrity had come out from their very first meeting, when he found her trying to clean a very upset Ruby out there in the cold.

He'd come to help then and had never stopped helping.

He smiled his tender, intimate smile, the one he reserved just for her. "That was us two weeks ago."

Had it only been two weeks? A very life-changing fortnight. She was nearly a different person now.

One who was treasured. Loved beyond what she'd ever allowed herself to imagine. By Sampson. By his family—her new family. And by God, the Father she'd been coming to know more every day.

She slipped her arm around Sampson's waist and leaned as close as she dared with his broken arm.

The deputy began the ceremony with the traditional opening, speaking about the sanctity and blessings of marriage. Blessings, indeed.

And she hadn't even experienced them all. Sampson had been so patient, waiting for her to be ready for the final step that would join them.

Gil was the first to speak his vows, as he held both of Jess's hands in his. Grace had never seen a man cry, but his voice broke as he promised to love and cherish her. She could only see Jess's face in profile, but her smile shone with the radiance of a woman fully loved.

Grace knew how that smile felt.

When it was Jonah's and Patsy's turn to speak their vows, Jonah sent his bride a wink as he started into his part. "I, Jonah Coulter, take thee, Patience Whitman, to be my lawfully wedded wife." Something in the way he spoke her name made it sound like there might be a story there.

Patsy's cheeks flushed a pretty pink.

He turned serious as he spoke the rest of the vows, but the joy never left his face. And when Patsy returned them, her voice rang rich and strong. These two had been waiting a while for this day.

The deputy concluded the ceremony giving the couples a moment to kiss.

Sampson turned to her with a twinkle in his eye. She didn't have to guess what he intended, and though their family stood all around, his idea was still a good one.

She rose up to meet his kiss. Somehow, Sampson could make the simple brushing of his lips over hers feel like fire that tingled all the way through her body.

When he pulled away, she opened her eyes to see he watched her with a smile. "We didn't get to do that on our wedding day. I have to make up for lost time." His eyes still held that twinkle, the one that made her belly flip.

Did she dare say what she really wanted to? Yes. This was the time.

She rose up on her toes to whisper in his ear. "There's something else we didn't get to do on our wedding day. I think it's time for that too."

When she lowered to the ground, his eyes stayed locked on hers. The twinkle had shifted to a question.

She met his gaze, letting her eyes say *yes*.

His rich brown orbs darkened to almost black. Then he swept in for another kiss. This one was even quicker than the first, but his intensity nearly made her knees buckle.

He shifted to murmur in her ear. "I love you, Grace Coulter."

Those five words filled her heart to overflowing. Every time.

She reached up to cup his warm cheek, her voice a whisper. "I love you, too, Sampson. More than I ever thought possible."

His eyes glistened with emotion as he pressed a tender kiss to her palm. The promise in that look, the depth of his commitment to her—it stole her breath.

The rest of the family started to disburse, heading back to the house for the meal.

She and Sampson turned to join them, and she let herself take in the scene.

Family. Love. Home. Every blessing she'd ever longed for, right here.

And she'd never stop being grateful.

EPILOGUE 2

My Dearest Eli,

As I watch you sleep in your cradle, I am filled with a love I never knew possible. Your tiny face, your perfect fingers curled around mine—I didn't realize until you arrived how much our family was missing. You have completed us in a way I couldn't have imagined.

I'm honored that God would entrust your mother and me with your care, with your safety. I know without a doubt we can only accomplish it with His grace.

There was a time when I feared losing control, when the weight of responsibility for our family felt almost too much to bear. But slowly, God showed me that He is trustworthy, that I need not carry these burdens alone. He has a plan, little one, for you and for all of us.

A plan for abundance beyond our hopes.

I've written down our family's stories, of the journeys and trials that brought us to where we are. The land has been divided now, freeing your uncles to follow the paths God has set before them. And you, my son—never be afraid to trust the Lord with your future. He will guide your steps, whether they lead you to the highest office in the land, or to a small ranch, surrounded by a loving wife and the laughter of your children.

I know you will do great things, son. You have a legacy of faith as your foundation, and a future bright with promise. No matter where life takes you, remember that your mother and I love you beyond measure, and that God holds you in the palm of His hand.

Your loving father,
Jericho

Did you enjoy Sampson and Grace's story? I hope so!
Would you take a quick minute to leave a review where you purchased the book?
It doesn't have to be long. Just a sentence or two telling what you liked about the story!

To receive a free book and get updates when new Misty M. Beller books release, go to https://mistymbeller.com/freebook

ALSO BY MISTY M. BELLER

Brothers of Sapphire Ranch

Healing the Mountain Man's Heart

Marrying the Mountain Man's Best Friend

Protecting the Mountain Man's Treasure

Earning the Mountain Man's Trust

Winning the Mountain Man's Love

Pretending to be the Mountain Man's Wife

Guarding the Mountain Man's Secret

Saving the Mountain Man's Legacy

Sisters of the Rockies

Rocky Mountain Rendezvous

Rocky Mountain Promise

Rocky Mountain Journey

The Mountain Series

The Lady and the Mountain Man

The Lady and the Mountain Doctor

The Lady and the Mountain Fire

The Lady and the Mountain Promise

The Lady and the Mountain Call

This Treacherous Journey

This Wilderness Journey

This Freedom Journey (novella)

This Courageous Journey

This Homeward Journey

This Daring Journey

This Healing Journey

Call of the Rockies

Freedom in the Mountain Wind

Hope in the Mountain River

Light in the Mountain Sky

Courage in the Mountain Wilderness

Faith in the Mountain Valley

Honor in the Mountain Refuge

Peace in the Mountain Haven

Grace on the Mountain Trail

Calm in the Mountain Storm

Joy on the Mountain Peak

Brides of Laurent

A Warrior's Heart

A Healer's Promise

A Daughter's Courage

Hearts of Montana

Hope's Highest Mountain

Love's Mountain Quest

Faith's Mountain Home

Honor's Mountain Promise

Texas Rancher Trilogy

The Rancher Takes a Cook

The Ranger Takes a Bride

The Rancher Takes a Cowgirl

Wyoming Mountain Tales

A Pony Express Romance

A Rocky Mountain Romance

A Sweetwater River Romance

A Mountain Christmas Romance